REDEMPTION
KEY

ALSO BY S.G. REDLING

The Widow File

Flowertown

Damocles

REDEMPTION KEY

A THRILLER BY

S.G. REDLING

PUBLISHED BY

THOMAS & MERCER

Published by Thomas & Mercer, Seattle

www.apub.com

Amazon, the Amazon logo, and Thomas & Mercer are trademarks of Amazon.com, Inc., or its affiliates.

ISBN-13: 9781477819609
ISBN-10: 1477819606

Cover design by becker&mayer! LLC

Library of Congress Control Number: 2013919786

Printed in the United States of America

For Gina Milum,
the best friend anyone could hope for

JINKY'S INLET FISHING CAMP, REDEMPTION KEY, FLORIDA

Wednesday, August 21
4:38am, 74° F

Dani lay on her back listening to the night sounds of the island, sensing the changing tide by the shifting breeze. She lay on the floating kayak dock, the rough indoor-outdoor carpet scratching her bare shoulders. In the hazy moonlight she could make out the shapes of date palms and sea grape around the inlet. No lights shone from the low buildings around her. Somewhere to her left, gravel crunched once, twice, and Dani tensed, turning her head to stare into the shadows. She didn't move. She didn't breathe.

The breeze shifted again, blowing clouds out of the way, letting moonlight fall on a pair of tiny Key deer picking their way across the parking lot. They lifted their heads, catching her scent, deciding if she was a threat. It seemed they didn't want to risk it and hurried along down the rutted road deeper into the island.

She knew how they felt. She knew that watchfulness.

At least now she was able to stay in one place, to keep herself from bolting into the darkness to find another place, a safer place, a place that wasn't where she was at the moment. There was no safer

1

place. She was her safest place. She stretched her left hand out to the edge of the bobbing dock and felt the warm water at her fingertips.

She was her safe zone, her only safe zone, and she knew how to defend it.

Dani sighed and sat up. No more sleep was coming tonight. And if it did she knew it would bring with it visions of blue eyes and strangling hands and she'd just claw her way out of the dream again. She woke up in a knot of sheets every night when the heat and the dreams overpowered her and only lying by the warm, still waters would soothe her.

Funny, she thought, that after nearly drowning, she loved being in the water more than ever. Of course, the warm tides of the islands were a far cry from the filthy, icy water of the Tidal Basin in Washington, DC. And she still had no memory of actually going into the water, just fevered ghosts of memories of hanging over the water, pain and terror suffocating her. They told her she had taken in a lungful of water, that she'd have drowned before she bled to death, that it was the iciness of the water that had saved her.

She didn't consciously remember the water but her body remembered the cold. Her core temperature had dropped dangerously low and now it seemed her body couldn't shake that chill. She could never be warm enough.

X X X

5:40am, 78° F

Oren would have checked his watch if he still wore one. As it was, his employee made as good a timepiece as the rising and setting sun. He peeled his tangerine, tossing the rinds into the water below the deck out back of his bar, and watched the sky brighten in the east. He squinted into the darker western horizon, toward the bridge over the open water, listening for the sound he'd come to expect. Right on time.

She'd gotten faster in the months since she'd started working for him. She ran hard and she ran fast and she never stopped for anything or anyone. She didn't even wave, not to him or anyone else on the island. He didn't mind. A person would have to be lacking some pretty basic survival instincts to want to intrude on the look in her eyes as she ran.

He remembered her labored breathing and stiff-legged limp those first few weeks. Back then he'd been sure she would give up the fight. You didn't have to be a doctor to recognize that big knot of scar tissue on her thigh. You didn't have to be a cop, either, to figure out what had caused it. The wide, ugly webbing of scars on her left shoulder was a little harder to explain, but Oren hadn't survived as long as he had by not knowing how to keep his curiosity in check.

He spit tangerine seeds over the railing as the pounding steps went silent on the middle of the bridge. In the pre-dawn haze, he could just make out her dark form against the sun-bleached concrete, the little light she clipped to her shorts flickering like a beacon. Late spring, early summer, when the sky brightened earlier, he would watch her stop on the bridge, bending and stretching, before she would stare down into the water.

The first time he'd seen what came next, he'd nearly shit himself.

With no preamble, she launched herself over the railing, falling feet first nearly fifteen feet into the channel.

He popped another segment of fruit into his mouth as he waited for her to resurface. She swam with the current today, crossing a hundred and twenty or so yards from the bridge to the dock below him. She alternated swimming styles; sometimes she swam with a strong, fast crawl, sometimes she'd return to his dock swimming most of the way underwater. Today was an underwater day. He'd watched her get better at that too. Once, he'd even tried to hold his breath the whole time she swam, but years of smoking all sorts of things had made that impossible.

He spit some more seeds and heard her splashing around below him. This was his favorite part. He eyed the crossbeam of the deck awning overhead as it creaked when a rope she'd tied there went taut and he resisted the urge to look over the railing. Of all the things he'd watched her struggle with, this seemed the most impossible. Seemed. It had taken weeks for her to clear the water and months before she'd taken her feet out of the effort. Now she barely even breathed hard as she pulled herself hand over hand up the rope, oblivious to the sea slime that slicked the way.

Water poured off of her body, her black tank top and black nylon shorts clinging to her as one brown hand after another gripped and pulled and climbed. She crossed her feet at the ankles, her entire body bent with the effort. She scraped her shoulder as she always did when she pulled herself over the railing of the deck, ignoring Oren and the water she flung around her. He let himself admire the tight curve of her ass when she twisted on the rope, lifting herself over his head, and watched her haul herself up all the way to the awning. Hey, he was old; he wasn't dead, and a man would have to be awfully close to the grave to not appreciate a sight like this. She pulled and twisted higher and higher until her head came level with the crossbeam.

She closed her eyes and pressed her forehead against the wooden beam, her mouth moving around words he couldn't hear over the breeze. She wrapped her legs around the rope, looping it around her feet to hold her weight. She slapped the beam with each hand. He wondered if her plan was to figure out a way to hold the rope with just her feet and slap the beam with both hands at once. It wouldn't surprise him, just like it wouldn't surprise him to see her achieve it.

Kicking her feet free, she loosened her grip and shimmied down the rope until her bottom landed on the railing. She was short and he smiled at the big leap she needed to make to land on the deck from the chest-high top rail. Only then did she acknowledge his presence and even then all he got was a nod. He handed her a tangerine.

"Thanks, boss." She pushed her thumb into the peel. He remembered how her hands used to shake after climbing off the rope.

"Sure thing, Dani. Gonna need you this morning for a meeting. The fucking Wheeler boys."

CHAPTER ONE

6:10am, 78°F

Dani liked her job here at Jinky's. She liked the busyness of it, the mindlessness of the work. She'd never seen a stranger set-up for an organization, and she'd never seen a bar open so early. Jinky's was a fishing camp on a mostly forgotten island in the Lower Keys. The little inlet took up less room than a football field, with slips to hold eight boats, maximum, at high season, which had passed two months before. Still, the bait shop and sundry store on the ground floor opened every morning at sixish, the bar above it opening right after to serve fishermen and kayakers and random hikers egg sandwiches and orange juice and beer to go. They served the locals rum drinks before dawn and mojitos to take the edge off the heat of the day, and if they were breaking any of the state's liquor laws, nobody saw the need to make a fuss.

It had been nine months since she'd left DC; almost six since she'd moved up from Key West, and the world she inhabited now felt lifetimes away from both. She'd fled to Key West, lured by the promise of being at the very farthest end of the continental US, just ninety miles from Cuba, all the signs promised. But when she got there, she felt no relief.

Part of her understood that she was the problem—that she couldn't shake the sense of being pursued, of being watched and hunted. She liked Key West, liked the live-and-let-live attitude of the crowded little island, but all those people kept her off-balance. Her weak shoulder and slowly ebbing limp made her feel vulnerable. The locals took her edginess in stride, the island being something of a haven for eccentrics of all stripes, but the tourists were a different story. They wanted chipper and charming; they wanted local color and expected her, as a waitress, to oblige with smiles and flirtation.

She did her best. Well, she did okay until one broad-chested man in a pack of broad-chested men had insisted on taking her picture with his cell phone. Once, she'd let it slide. Twice, and she asked him to stop. By the sixth time he'd waved that phone in her face, clicking and clicking and laughing and hooting, the edges of Dani's vision had gone dark. When she'd heard the phones of the men around her chirping at the arrival of her picture in their message boxes, she'd found it hard to hear much more.

And when the photographer put his hand on the back of her neck? She still didn't remember what had happened after that. She just knew it ended up with his broken nose and her unemployment. Dani knew she had to leave.

And so she'd driven north, the only direction available to her. She drove over bridge after bridge, over channels and through Keys with names like Boca Chica and Summerland, Sugarloaf, Shark, and Ramrod. She gripped the wheel tightly, back in survival mode, willing her mind to corral her thoughts, to line them up into manageable compartments. It was a skill she'd acquired as a child, the ability to segment her thoughts. That skill had gotten her the job at Rasmund and that skill had kept her alive when hell rained down on her last

November. By the time she pulled onto Big Pine Key, she'd willed herself into a tear-inducing headache. By the time she pulled into the parking lot of the Walgreens, her hands shook so badly she could barely turn off the car.

When she'd pulled back out and continued driving, she couldn't face the early spring traffic, so she'd turned left instead of right, went farther into the island than through it, and found herself following signs for the Key Deer Refuge. That sounded better than miles of tourists on a highway with nothing but the rest of the United States ahead of her, so she'd let herself drift along narrow roads sheltered and shadowed with bougainvillea and date palms. One turn after another, she tried and succeeded at getting lost. That's when she came to the crossroad.

If she went left, if she followed the state-manufactured sign, she would be on No Name Key. That sounded good. But if she went right, if she followed a faded wooden sign that pointed down a rutted, narrow road, she would find Redemption.

That sounded better.

So Dani Britton had rolled her sixteen-year-old Honda over the concrete bridge and onto the gravel-covered property of Jinky's Fishing Camp not fifteen minutes after a water heater had ruptured in one of the little rental units. A white-haired man in his late fifties had handed her a mop while swearing a blue streak, and six months later, here she was. The white-haired man was Mr. Oren Randolph, and her job description included maid, handyman, waitress, bait slinger, and kayak wrangler. She worked from before sunrise to long after dark. She started running, letting her body heal and strengthen. She moved into the ratty little kayak shed with the outdoor toilet and shower after Mr. Randolph caught her sleeping in her car, and she'd finally managed to find the right balance of vitamin A and Skin So Soft bath oil to keep the mosquitoes from killing her.

She thought that maybe she was happy.

X X X

Since there were still a few fishermen renting units, Peg, the night bartender, had decided to work the bait counter this morning. Dani knew that, like Rolly in the kitchen, the tough woman made her own schedule, regardless of Mr. Randolph's orders. That was about the only thing the two long-term employees had in common. Peg kept her bleached-to-death hair piled in a tattered knot on top of her head, revealing faded tattoos along her creased neck and bony shoulders. Her skin had the leathery look fair-skinned people got after decades in the too-hot sun. Even skin cancer wasn't tough enough to take on Peg. Rolly, on the other hand, acted as if the sun would set him on fire, covering every inch of his dark, baby-smooth skin during all daylight hours.

Dani slipped behind the counter as Peg brought a huge cleaver down onto a mess of baitfish.

"You're dripping."

Dani nodded. She'd rinsed off with the hose outside the bait shop; the water coming off her running clothes would just drain out with the fish muck. What didn't make it to the drain would be forced along when Peg did her usual cleanup of the place. Mr. Randolph declared Jinky's décor 'hurricane chic,' and Peg kept it up by cleaning both levels in the afternoons by turning the hose onto every surface regardless of whether a person occupied it. Tourists considered it a charming affectation. Dani knew Peg hoped they wouldn't be fast enough to avoid the spray.

Dani and Peg got along very well.

With a quick check to be sure nobody could see her, Dani pulled her wet clothes off and pulled out the rubber tub of dry clothes she kept there. Underwear, bra, and whatever sat on top of the pile. Today it was a black golf shirtdress. That was good. The heat wave they'd been promised seemed to be delivering, but Dani always felt better with a little fabric between her and the Wheeler boys. She tossed her wet running clothes onto the porch behind the bait shop and headed back up to prep the bar for the few morning customers.

Of course she'd had the option of not working at all for a while. She still had almost forty thousand dollars from her previous life squirreled away. Nobody knew about that money, she was certain. The people who had taken everything from her had a special fondness for cash. They weren't likely to have let her keep it, so the less she relied on that money, the better. Unlike many people who fled to the Keys for a new life, Dani Britton didn't want to drop off the map entirely. She couldn't, not for a while at least. Dani needed to obtain legal, taxable employment, create a nice solid paper trail of nice solid citizenship because Dani knew she was still 'a person of interest' to more than one government agency.

Did they think she didn't know about the tracking device in her car, her much-beloved maroon Accord, now parked under the carport on the edge of the lot? Their opinion of her couldn't be that low, especially since they had been so certain she'd been involved in the whole sick Rasmund mess.

Dani plunged the knife into the first of a dozen oranges, stabbing harder than necessary to cut the fruit, not a fraction hard enough to vent her anger. Six years ago she had taken a job with what she thought was a private investigation firm only to find out it had been a front for an agency of the United States government. That same government claimed to know nothing of the agency's existence when hired forces had descended upon them to wipe them out. Her friends had been murdered; she had been shot and nearly drowned. Nobody took the blame for the deaths; nobody took the blame for the crimes committed under that roof.

After three months of painful surgery and recuperation, to say nothing of terrifying interrogation in a classified facility, Dani had stepped back into a world in which it seemed nobody had even noticed the atrocities committed in their backyard. Nobody paid any price at all except her and the dead.

And Choo-Choo.

Another orange, another savage slice, and Dani bit back the emotion she couldn't identify. Anger? Fear? Regret? She didn't know. Gorgeous, silly, funny Sinclair "Choo-Choo" Charbaneaux—she had left him in that place. He'd taken a bullet for her and she had left him in that place. She hadn't had much of a choice—he probably had months of recovery ahead of him, his wounds much more severe than hers. Plus her choices had been made for her from the moment they pulled her from the icy water of the Tidal Basin. When they told her to sleep, she slept. When they told her to talk, she spit out every single word her mouth could manage. And when they were done with her, they had bundled her into a windowless van and dumped her outside her apartment with five thousand dollars cash and the keys to her car, and a very clear directive to never utter a word about the previous five years of her life.

So now she made mojitos and cleaned toilets and sold baitfish. And she paid taxes. Mr. Randolph had been surprised by that last part, but she knew she'd made the right decision. She had a roof over her head, warm water to swim in. She ran and nobody chased her. Most importantly, she had a legal, traceable stream of income to report obediently to the Internal Revenue Service, letting the powers that be know she was holding up her end of the devil's bargain they'd offered her.

XXX

6:48am, 83° F

Oren unlocked the cash register and flipped on the ceiling fans. He didn't bother with the overhead lights. It was already hot, and anyone headed to Jinky's at this hour didn't need lights to find their way.

They could hear Rolly humming to himself in the kitchen as he prepped for breakfast.

"Is Peg going to cover the bar for you during the meeting?" Oren asked. "You know how Joaquin likes you to serve him his drinks."

Dani rolled her eyes and nodded. Oren laughed.

He had taken over Jinky's from his former coke dealer when the man had decided to flee the country. Along with all the fixtures, the booze, and the debt, he'd inherited Jinky's former girlfriend Peg as a waitress and Rolly, the short-order cook. That was seventeen years ago, and both Peg and Rolly had stayed on, keeping their own hours, setting their own pay. Oren didn't mind. Finding good help in the transient population of the islands wasn't easy. Besides, he was scared of Peg, and even after all these years he wasn't sure what Rolly's real name was or even where he lived. Sometimes life in the Keys was like that.

Dani fit in like she was born to it. First of all, the regulars were so used to the disdain of Peg, the younger woman seemed like a ray of sunshine in comparison. At least she didn't throw the drinks onto the table. And while it had been more than a decade and a half since coke accounted for the majority of the bar's profits, the clientele hadn't become overly reputable. Jinky's maintained its aura of slightly shady, slightly rough local watering hole, frequented by the type of drinkers who like their bartenders on the less engaging side.

There were always exceptions, especially during high season. More than half of the season visitors were yearly regulars—fishermen and snorkelers, stoners and hippies, who liked to get away from the commercialism of the other Keys. What they didn't realize was that their presence created the very commercialism they were trying to escape, but the locals accepted them—and their money—with a fair amount of equilibrium. Two-thirds of Oren's rooms had been booked from February through June, and the season had been lucrative.

"Don't forget," Dani said, rinsing off a bowl of lemons, "the Texans are checking out of Five today."

"Any chance they'll take the Australians with them?" A group of Australians in Room Six had broken the two windows and the air-conditioner, and backed up the toilet at least every other week since taking the place at the end of June. "You might as well close off the rest of the cottages after the Texans go. We probably won't need any rooms but the four in the unit across the way, and even those'll be mostly for meetings." Except for an isolated weekend here or there, Jinky's rental units would be at a near standstill, tourist-wise, until November.

Oren had foolishly thought he could cut Dani from the payroll at the end of the season. He'd even told Peg that, only to face her braying laugh. She'd known all along that he'd never have the heart to throw the strange, quiet girl out. More than once Oren wondered who was actually running this joint.

Dani had proven herself valuable in more ways than one. For one thing, she seemed impossible to gross out. Fish heads and backed-up toilets, dead rats and vomiting kids, nothing made her flinch. Plus she could rig up fixes for the endless list of breakdowns in the old camp. Windows, air-conditioners, even the listing kayak dock—she'd pick through the old toolboxes and rescue bits of metal and wood from the debris pile hidden behind the clump of sea grape at the water's edge and cobble together a workable and inexpensive solution.

She didn't take up any room. When he'd found her sleeping in her car, he'd told her to fix up the kayak shack until she could make other arrangements. Since she had access to the master key for the units, Oren had assumed she would make herself at home in one of the cottages, sneaking her linens in and out with the renters'. But no, she'd repaired a crappy old cot, wired in some screens, and scrubbed out an old beer fridge. She'd asked permission to use rental sheets, to park her car under the carport, even to hang that rope from the upper deck of Jinky's. Why she'd wanted to keep her clothes in a rubber tub in the bait shop was beyond him, but if it didn't bother Peg, why fight it?

But where she really sealed her place at Jinky's was at his meetings. He'd been glad to have her serve drinks at his meetings rather than Peg. Dani was small and unthreatening, cute but not overly so. She kept her eyes down and her mouth shut and moved so quietly and efficiently, people often forgot she was there.

If they only knew.

The first meeting she'd served had been between Angel Jackson and some Ohio gangster wannabe who wanted the black-eyed pilot to help him move some weed through the Keys. Oren had sat back, letting the two men hash out the details, until Dani had asked him to step outside with her. She'd told him the Ohioan was lying, and his money was fake. She'd been so blunt and dispassionate about it, so confident, that Oren had gone right in, upended the dealer's bag and discovered that all but the top layer of cash bundles were cut newspaper wrapped in hundred-dollar bills.

He'd let Angel handle the rest.

Oren didn't ask how Dani had known, and she hadn't offered. But he'd had her serve every meeting since, even ones with the Wheelers.

X X X

On the neighboring Keys, even as far up as Miami, Oren Randolph was known as "that guy." When someone needed a set of fake IDs good enough to get through customs, they called Oren. If they needed a connection to certain groups of influence, they called Oren. Technically, Oren bought and sold nothing but drinks and seafood, but he was the guy who knew the guy who sold the things, legal and not, that people needed. And he had a reputation for discretion as well as connections to smooth over the more questionable transactions on many levels. Oren thought of himself as a resource manager, an information broker.

The Wheeler boys were an unfortunate third-generation inheritance that came with Jinky's. Juan and Joaquin Wheeler probably weren't brothers in anything other than their full-fledged psychosis.

Their major business consisted of smuggling and bloodshed from Miami to Key West. They had overthrown the previous psychopath who had controlled the heroin traffic, said psychopath being the man who had so unnerved Jinky as to cause the coke dealer to run for his life to points unknown. Before that unlikely event, Oren Randolph had considered Jinky to be the most dangerously deranged human he had ever known.

Seventeen years and many, many horrific tales later Oren's horizons had broadened.

As always, Dani seemed to read his mind. "Looking forward to another chance to get chummy with Juan Wheeler?"

Oren shook his head. "Trust me. Nobody does business with the Wheelers by choice. Luckily for me, they seem to hold me in something of a favored, protected light—some Wheeler combination of elder worship and historic preservation." He slammed the register shut. "I don't care if they put me on an endangered species list; they haven't killed me or anyone dear to me."

"Yet."

"Yet. But hey"—he nudged her and gave her a wink—"I think Joaquin has got his eye on you. His good one, that is."

Dani laughed. Oren liked the sound of it. Quiet little stone-faced Dani handled the clumsy passes and drool—yes, actual drool—with finesse. Joaquin still ogled, she still served him, and all of them kept breathing.

For now.

That the Wheelers had come to him needing a connection had been bad enough; when they told him with pride that they were orchestrating a deal for Simon Vincente, a known butcher, arms dealer, and all around tornado of evil throughout the entire state of Florida, he'd almost balked. Almost. But everyone knew that anyone saying no to Vincente usually got as far as "Nuh" before losing at least one favored body part.

The only upside in the dismal deal was that Vincente and the Wheelers knew exactly who they were looking for, just not how to find him. That's why they came to Oren, trusting that his contacts ran deep. So he'd called around and found their man—a Canadian gangster named Bermingham. Oren learned the man was a butcher in his own right who had ways to grease the wheels of Canadian customs, and a habit of creating scenes that needed bleach to clean up.

Terrific.

He didn't know who was selling what to whom, and he wanted to keep it that way. But Bermingham had insisted the meeting take place before ten in the morning, and Juan Wheeler always liked to be an hour or two early for meetings. That didn't give Oren much time to contact the FBI.

CHAPTER TWO

Oren fished his phone from his pocket and dialed Caldwell's number from memory. As usual, he heard the sound of feminine giggling before the agent spoke.

"This had better be important." Caldwell's voice sounded thick with sleep.

"If you had called me back last night, you'd have known that the Wheelers are coming in today."

He heard something slapping flesh and a high-pitched squeal. "I was busy last night."

"Well we're all going to be busy today. Let's talk."

"Where are you?"

"Where do you think I am?" Oren climbed onto his usual barstool. "I'd wager I'm a hell of a lot closer to my office than you are to yours."

"That goes without saying." Caldwell groaned into the phone. "Give me twenty minutes. And I'm putting my drinks on your tab."

"That goes without saying too, doesn't it?"

"Not too early for a mojito, is it?"

"Is it ever?"

XXX

7:40am, 86° F

Caldwell sat where he always sat, next to Oren's stool at the short end of the bar. Strictly speaking, that section of the bar was service only, but since Rolly tossed most of the food through the window and Peg had never been overly committed to the service aspect of the job, Caldwell had claimed that section as his own private perch. Caldwell's receding hairline shone with sweat and his pink guayabera shirt brought out the sea of freckles that covered every inch of his exposed skin. He was in the middle of telling Peg a story that made the normally cross woman pitch her head back and howl. Oren could only imagine how filthy the punch line had to be to elicit that reaction.

"Well take your time, son!" Caldwell took his drink from Oren. "It's not like I have all day to sit here and get hit on by your staff."

"You wish," Peg said, slapping a bowl of peanuts down before the agent.

"You know I do, Peg. You know I do. Anytime you want to take me up on it . . ." He lunged across the bar, swinging and missing a chance to swat Peg's behind as she turned away from him, still laughing. Caldwell was the only person in all of Florida Oren had met who could get the hard woman to laugh like that.

Special Agent Daniel Caldwell worked out of the Miami FBI office but spent most of his times cruising the Keys. He claimed it was his territory, but Oren knew Caldwell spent more time investigating the evolution of the mojito than he did the influx of drugs and guns across state lines. Not that he was crooked exactly, any more than Oren himself. As the agent liked to say, he had a broad understanding of the nature of business. He'd come through more than once for Oren over the years, distracting local law enforcement when Oren struggled to get his coke use under control, and Oren had repaid the favor many times over. Caldwell had a weakness for wealthy women and volatile girls—a lethal combination—and had needed a place to hide more than once.

Caldwell always wanted to be kept distantly informed about the Wheelers. He wouldn't meddle, Oren knew. He wouldn't stage a bust at Jinky's or bring any hint of law enforcement into Oren's sphere of influence. He also let Oren know right away if any of his clients were misrepresenting themselves—men who claimed to be boat collectors who were actually mob enforcers; alleged diamond dealers moving large quantities of heroin. The exchange of information benefitted both Caldwell and Oren, keeping them both in good standing in their respective fields. Plus, Oren liked the crabby little agent. He was a hell of a fisherman.

Oren had told himself he was going to stick to orange juice this morning, but the combination of the Wheelers' impending arrival and the sound of Caldwell sighing over his mojito made him change his mind. Peg had taken her bucket of ice back down to the bait shop so Oren called to Dani, who stood at the far end of the bar prepping fruit, as she always did in the morning. It was just too hot to get up again. "Dani? How about a vodka?"

She scraped the limes into the bin and wiped her hands on her towel. "Sure thing, boss." She knew how he liked his drink—lots of ice, one lime wedge squeezed to death—and slid it before him in no time. Oren watched her small, tan hands settle on the bar, just a fraction of a second of a delay that seemed to him an act of composure, before she raised her gaze to Caldwell and scared the hell out of Oren.

She smiled. It wasn't a big smile; it wasn't shark-like. She didn't leer, and her eyes didn't glare coldly above her bare teeth. It was just the smile of a girl working a bar for tips, but it looked sort of wrong on Dani's face.

"How's your drink, sir? Can I get you anything?"

Caldwell turned to Oren in comic shock. "Sir? I know it's been a while since I've been in, but has it been that long? Have you insti-tuted new house rules?"

Oren dismissed his anxiety. "You haven't met my new wonder girl? Dani Britton, I'd like to introduce you to a man you must never let touch you. Daniel Caldwell or, as Peg calls him, Uncle Bad Touch."

Caldwell bowed at the introduction and flashed Dani his signa-ture lady-killer smile. "Don't believe a word of it, sweetheart. I'm a scholar and a gentleman. Hey, we're Dan and Dani. We could start a dance team." He winked at her. "What do you say?"

Dani kept that strange smile in place but said nothing. Oren thought her eyes looked a lot like they did when she was climbing the rope. Caldwell continued, unfazed.

"So where are you from, Dani?"

Her lips whitened around the edges and Oren spoke up. "Okla-homa. Dani started out doing housekeeping and when Hesson got arrested, she stepped up and never looked back. She makes a mean mojito, you'll be happy to hear. Better than mine."

"You're keeping her hidden from me? You lecherous bastard. I do like my mojitos." Caldwell beamed at Dani, who hadn't moved an inch. "And if I may say so, you are a vast improvement over Hes-son in the looks department. Let's hope you're a little less larcenous too. Or at least a better judge of targets."

"Poor Hesson." Oren lifted his glass in salute. "Never did have a lick of sense."

Dani watched them drink, her hands still folded on the bar. "If there's nothing else, Mr. Randolph, I'm going to finish prepping the bar; then I'll set up the room."

"Thank you, Dani." Oren watched her over his drink as she moved down the bar.

Caldwell watched her too, his focus on her ass. He arched an eyebrow. "Something you'd like to tell me? Like, are you hitting that? Because I have to say, making your piece call you sir takes some balls."

"Do you practice being a pig, or does it just come naturally?"

He ignored the barb to watch Dani. "She's a little thing, isn't she? What's her story?"

Oren shrugged. "She's not much of a talker. She can run like hell, I'll tell you that. She runs the island every single day. Good worker, too. Keeps her mouth shut. Does her job." He opted not to mention her helpfulness during his meetings.

"What do you think?" The agent crunched an ice cube in his open mouth. "Bad breakup? I've seen her around the property. She doesn't seem inclined to make new friends. She's ducked me a couple times. She ever pick anyone up?"

"Jealous?" Something in Caldwell's tone made Oren want to change the subject.

"You said she runs. Maybe she's been running a long time. You think Dani Britton is her real name?"

"If it's not, it's a hell of a cover. She's legal, paid aboveboard. She insisted on it." Under-the-table employment shocked nobody in this part of the country, not even a federal agent.

"Insisted, huh?" Another ice cube shattered in his mouth. "Why would she do that?"

"Because it's required by law? And she's a good citizen?" Oren sipped his vodka. "Look, I've got Rolly in the kitchen who has been shot no less than three times, at least once by Peg, who scares the hell out of everyone from here to Miami, including the alligators. I'm pleased as punch to finally have a legitimate employee on the payroll, one with half a brain."

Caldwell's voice took on a low and serious tone. "I'm not saying she's bad news. I'm just saying you should know a little more about her."

"What? I've got the Wheelers coming in and *she* makes you suspicious? It's not like she moved in with a drug-sniffing dog. She's a five-foot-nothing girl who keeps her mouth shut and does her job."

"Then there's no harm in running a background check."

Oren emptied his glass. "I think the reason you don't like her is because she doesn't like you. She's impervious to your devious charms."

Caldwell shook his head at Oren's smirk. "You have such a low opinion of me."

XXX

Dani wiped her hands twice on the towel. She'd nearly cut her fingertip off, her hands shook so badly. She had promised to work the Wheeler meeting. She knew Mr. Randolph appreciated her ability to stay calm around the twitchy men who made everyone at Jinky's nervous. Even Peg avoided them. She couldn't say she liked them— she doubted anyone could—but they didn't scare her. Even when wall-eyed Joaquin tried to slip his hand between her legs, she didn't panic. She knew what he wanted and that made him easier to handle. A lot easier to handle than what sat at the end of the bar.

Caldwell. The very first time Dani had laid eyes on the balding man, the very first time she'd seen him climb onto the barstool and fold his arms over the lip of the wood, she'd known who he was. She'd known what he was. Dani's employment by a government agency might have been unintentional, but she could recognize a willing employee of the state at a hundred paces.

He didn't usually carry a gun, although Dani had spied the ungainly bulge at his back once or twice. He didn't wear the ugly suits that seemed to be regulation for many Feds. He didn't even flash his badge around like an extension of his dick.

What gave him away to Dani was the smug confidence that followed him like a smell, confidence that he had authority, immunity, the ability to arrest, and the security of never being arrested. The arrogance of authority showed itself in every peanut he tossed back, every filthy joke he told.

At first she assumed he was yet another agent sent to check on her like they had on Key West. That never seemed to get old for Uncle

Sam. Sometimes the agent or agents made a show of their presence, full suits and dark glasses, standing too close to her and looking down their badges at her. Sometimes they tried to slide in like locals, looking ridiculous in their idea of vacation clothing. They'd try to make idle chitchat with her. After the first few visits she realized they were just there to remind her that she was still in their sights.

She still hated them. She still had to resist the urge to run. She'd avoided Caldwell as long as possible but she knew she'd wind up having to serve the balding agent his drink. She'd have to let him run his line of patter that would inevitably end with "You being a good girl, Dani?" to which he would expect her to faint in terror. She thought she'd hide her eye roll and that would be the end of it. Then Mr. Randolph had shown up, slapped the man on the back and sat down for a lengthy, friendly conversation.

And Dani was stuck there with the man watching her like he thought if he stared hard enough he'd be able to see right through her. What did they tell her babysitters? Surely not the truth. From what Dani had been able to tell, nobody knew the truth about Rasmund. So why was Caldwell so interested in her?

"I'm going to go set up the room, boss."

Mr. Randolph wanted a basic wet bar setup in Room Four, just the basics—glasses, ice, napkins, garnishes. Dani would run the liquor and the mixes herself. She knew his logic—her occasional interruptions served as punctuation to the meeting's rhythm. Her boss used her service as an unspoken reminder that he controlled the scene. If tempers got hot, he'd break in with a suggestion of fresh drinks; if stony silence threatened to stall discussions, he'd send Dani to fetch food. He'd even smoothed over one potentially violent face-off by having Dani pour tequila poppers. Mr. Randolph knew how to control a room.

"Be sure to get the fan going," Mr. Randolph said. "I don't know what this Bermingham guy smells like, but in this heat, you can pretty much bet the Wheelers are going to reek."

Dani would sooner be locked naked in a windowless room with every Wheeler in Florida than spend one more moment under the eye of a Fed.

X X X

8:05am, 85° F

"Hot enough for you?" Caldwell asked.

"It's August in Florida," Oren said.

"Yeah but it's not even nine o'clock and it's got to be ninety degrees already. That's not Florida hot. That's Vietnam hot. That's gunplay-in-the-streets hot."

"Don't remind me."

Caldwell pulled a mint leaf from his glass. "Any idea what the deal is?"

"Bancroft told me it was antiques." Oren poked at the lime rind that stuck to the side of the glass. Bancroft was the fence who had hooked him up with the Canadian. "He said there might be some concerns over provenance but that the goods were top shelf, top dollar."

"Bancroft has never told the truth in his whole miserable life," Caldwell said. "You thinking drugs?"

"It's the Wheelers, so yeah, you'd think so. But with Vincente in the mix, who knows?"

Caldwell nodded. "And this Bermingham guy, you know him?"

"No, I was hoping you could give me some skinny on him. Bancroft got his connection thirdhand from the truck boys in Miami. They worked with a guy who worked with him. He's an unknown at this point. The little I do know makes Vincente sound like a missionary."

"Any idea what the dollar figure is for the deal?"

"Significant. That's all Juan Wheeler said. And if it's big enough for him to keep his mouth shut on the take, it's either embarrassingly small or large enough to buy his silence. Either way, I'm getting the usual stack for my hospitality."

The two men sat in silence, swirling the ice in their glasses in accidental synchronization. "I'll run a check on the Canadian, usual discreet channels. While I'm at it, I'll check on your faithful new employee."

Oren said nothing. He and Caldwell knew each other too well. If Oren protested the background check, it would just make the agent more curious. If he encouraged it, Caldwell might think Oren agreed with his instinct and dig deeper than absolutely necessary. Oren didn't know if Dani had anything in her background worth hiding. It could be she'd run from an abusive home or a drug problem. He also didn't know if Caldwell had seen the scars on her leg and shoulder. They'd be sure to pique the agent's interest.

What unsettled him the most, however, wasn't the odd pitch of Caldwell's curiosity. It was the memory of that strange smile on Dani's face. He had the feeling that of the three of them, he was the only one not seeing something obvious.

A warm breeze blew in from the deck, and Oren wrinkled his nose at the smell. Sour feet and onions. It wasn't a smell he was likely to mistake.

"Why don't you take the front stairs?" He drained his drink and nodded toward the kitchen door. "It looks like Juan wants to get a jump on things."

Caldwell fished an ice cube out with his fingers and tossed it in his mouth. "I appreciate your discretion. I don't need to tell you to keep your eyes open and your guard up. If Vincente wants this Bermingham guy bad enough to get into bed with the Wheelers, odds are nobody's got anything good in mind."

CHAPTER THREE

Smelling Juan Wheeler before seeing him was nothing unusual. Both Wheelers carried an unmistakable funk about them at all times. The heat didn't help. The little man took his usual seat on the deck of Jinky's with his back against the outer wall of the bar, staring at the stairs that came up from the dock. He wore a stained Marlins T-shirt with shiny black dress pants and his signature accessory—neon sneakers. Today's were pink. Oren didn't know if anyone had ever survived telling him that his footwear selections were often from the girl's department. His right hand rested on his lap, Oren knew within easy reach of his Glock.

The breeze shifted, blowing in from the open water to the left, and Oren could smell Joaquin. He smelled a lot like his brother only with added notes of cigarettes and bacon. Oren didn't bother to look where Juan stared. Joaquin would be blocking the top of the outer steps, using his lumpish form to keep anyone from joining them on the deck.

Everything about the Wheelers was bad for business.

"Good morning, Juan." Oren pulled up a seat.

"How you doing?" The high pitch of Juan's voice never failed to surprise Oren. He suspected that, like the little man's shoe selection,

26

few people survived mocking it. Juan sprawled back in his chair, folding his arms up over his head to catch the breeze, amping up the unpleasant smell. The only plus side to that from Oren's perspective was that it might keep the breeze from scattering the grainy flecks of dandruff that clung to Juan's greasy brown hair.

He wished he'd refreshed his drink.

"Everything is set up for the meeting this morning. On my end at least. You'll be in Room Four." Oren nodded across the inlet to a long, low cinder block unit with four doors. Unlike the four little cottages across the parking lot at the short end of the horseshoe, Oren kept the cinder block units open and ready all year. The cottages were for tourists and fishermen during high season. The cinder block units were for business associates. He'd found the cinder block walls did more to muffle sound and stop bullets than drywall. "You're early. I told Bermingham nine-thirty."

"Yeah." Juan smiled, doing little to improve his looks. He started to laugh, a high-pitched chittering that forced him to drop his arms. "About that. There might be a change of plans."

"Is that such a good idea? It wasn't easy to find this guy."

"Yeah. Yeah." The smile widened, and Oren felt a sick twist in his stomach from more than the sight of Juan's yellowed teeth. "Mr. Vincente is working out the details. Mr. Vincente is aware of how important this deal is to our Canadian friend."

"The less I know the better."

Juan slid his hands underneath the table, shifting to reach inside the waistband of his dress pants. He pulled out a stained manila envelope, which he slid across to Oren.

"Mr. Vincente said to tell you how much he appreciates your help with this matter."

Oren stared at the envelope that had been housed in Juan's underwear. Filthy money in the truest sense of the word. "With all due respect to Mr. Vincente, my help in this matter ends with setting up this meeting."

"Yeah," Juan chittered again. "About that. That's part of the change of plans."

Heavy clomping on the steps distracted him from continuing. Oren saw what made the oafish Wheeler guarding the steps stumble. He could just make out the top of Dani's head as Joaquin pressed himself hard against the wooden stair rail, great lumps of him squeezing through the slats, to wave Dani through with a swing of his meaty arm.

He didn't know how she managed to keep her composure, but Dani just gave the hulking man a small smile and squeezed past him onto the deck. Oren didn't want to think about what Joaquin Wheeler must smell like at armpit level.

"Hey, Dani," Juan said, smiling at his brother. "Good to see you."

"Yeah, Dani," Joaquin wheezed, tugging on the hem of his sweat-stained shirt, effectively highlighting even more of his odd frame. His eyes moved over Dani. "Good to see you."

She kept her back to Joaquin. She had to know he was staring at her ass. "Can I get anyone a drink?"

"Oh God, yes," Oren sighed.

XXX

Dani snuck a quick glance into the bar. Caldwell was gone. That was good. She didn't believe in coincidences, though. A federal agent and the Wheeler boys didn't just happen to show up on the same day before nine in the morning. Had Caldwell's arrival been a surprise to her boss? Or was it supposed to be a secret from the Wheelers? Either way, it wasn't her problem. If her boss wanted to play both sides of whatever this deal was, he would play it without her.

FBI versus the Wheelers. Dani would have been hard-pressed to deem one side less likeable than the other.

She'd felt Joaquin's gun when she'd squeezed past him. At least she prayed that was a gun. She'd been so focused on making as little body contact as possible, not just to avoid the feel-up but because she really didn't want to wear Joaquin's unique fragrance on her clothes the rest of the morning. The temperatures were supposed to soar today with the humidity right behind it. Nothing was going to get any sweeter this afternoon.

"Juan?" She waited for the smaller Wheeler to break the giggling eye contact he held with his brother. Judging from the way Mr. Randolph looked elsewhere, she could just imagine the expression on Joaquin's face. "Can I get you something?"

"You got Mexi-Coke? You know? Coke from Mexico?"

"We do."

"Good. Good." Juan drummed his fingers on the table. "It's made with real sugar, you know that? Real sugar, not that-that-that chemical stuff they use up here. Real sugar."

Dani doubted Juan and chemicals had ever been strangers. "Ice?"

"Two. Yeah, two cubes." He held up two grimy fingers just in case she didn't understand the words. He always ordered the same thing—Mexican coke with two ice cubes. Dani knew the specific order made the little man feel like a connoisseur of soft drinks and the better Juan felt about himself, the smoother and briefer his meetings tended to go. She nodded and turned back to Joaquin, slowly enough to give him time to pull his gaze up from her ass. No matter how slowly she turned, however, she was always too quick.

"Joaquin?" She saw a flush rise beneath his pocked skin. His good eye flickered toward her face and then away. "Can I get you something to drink?"

"Same. Same." Spit flew as he stammered.

"Two Mexican cokes with ice and another vodka. Be right back."

"We'll be right here," Juan cackled.

She caught the long-suffering look on her boss's face. Maybe it was the heat, maybe it was the scent of the Wheelers, but the look sent a spark of irritation through her.

No, she knew what irritated her. "Is your friend joining you, boss?"

She tipped her head toward the bar, where he and Caldwell had been moments before. Mr. Randolph's eyes widened for just a second before he shook his head.

"Nah, it's just us. That was just an old fishing buddy passing through."

Juan didn't seem to catch the muffled anxiety in his voice. Mr. Randolph was a better-than-average liar, a skill more difficult than most people understood. Dani graced him with the same noncommittal nod she'd given the Wheelers, and she could see him studying her face as she moved past him.

X X X

8:37am, 87° F

Jesus Christ. Oren thought his heart would leap from his chest when Dani asked him about Caldwell. Peg might have her suspicions that his buddy was with the FBI, her ability to sense law enforcement honed by years of living in fear of it, but Caldwell always made a point of keeping his head down and his badge out of sight. Oren could think of about a thousand other things he'd rather be discussing in front of the Wheelers. Safe to say, the Wheelers would not be amused at Caldwell's occupation.

Bless her heart but Dani had shitty timing.

He jumped back into conversation as she headed into the bar. "So what's this change of plan? I didn't agree to anything else but setting up the meeting."

"That's all you got to do," Juan said, pulling out a cheap-looking phone. "Set up this meeting and a couple others. You know, this deal is going to take some negotiating. Gimme Bermingham's number."

Oren pulled out the slip of paper he'd been carrying with him since his contact in Miami had passed it on to him. It was just like Juan to expect him to play secretary. He'd only called the Canadian twice, both times from the payphone outside the Winn-Dixie shopping center on Big Pine Key. He didn't need anyone to trace the calls back to him. The odds were that the number only went to a burner phone, but Oren figured nobody ever regretted being too careful.

Juan punched the number into his phone, settling back in his seat and giving Oren a wink. Oren hated winks. Nothing good ever followed a wink.

"Yeah, yeah, how you doing?" Juan smirked as he spoke. "This is in regards to our meeting this morning. Mr. Vincente is making some fine-tuning adjustments to the arrangement."

Juan sat up straighter, and Oren could make out an angry tone coming from the phone.

"No, you don't make the terms, see? Mr. Vincente, he makes the terms. He sets the deal. He's got the goods, you toe the line. You got it?" The little man spit when he spoke. "You don't like the deal, I take our product elsewhere. What's that?" More shouting and Juan pulled the phone away from his ear to glare at it.

Great, Oren thought as the sun cleared the trees across the road, falling hot and bright on the deck. Now everybody's pissed.

"I'm here with Randolph," Juan said, nodding to Oren as if checking to see if he was in fact here with him. "I'm going to go over the new plans. You listening? The deal isn't happening today." Oren could just make out something shouted on the other end, hearing a lot of words that sounded like *duck*. "How many ways I got to tell you this, huh? This isn't your deal to decide. Mr. Vincente has the product; Mr. Vincente makes the rules. That's how it is. Also: Now we're doing the exchange right here, right here at Jinky's."

"What?" Oren leaned forward. Juan smiled at him and nodded.

"Yeah, yeah, here. Google it. They got Google in Canada, right?" Juan spared a moment to point at Joaquin, who thought that line was a lot funnier than Oren did. Oren tried not to notice the spit that rained down from the bigger Wheeler's laughing mouth. He was glad the sun had hit the deck. It would hopefully dry up the glob of wetness near his foot.

"I'll keep you apprised of the new terms." Juan nodded at Oren again, impressed with his own vocabulary. "Tomorrow morning, same time, same channel. Oh, and Bermingham, if you're thinking about trying anything like trying to nickel-and-dime Mr. Vincente, trust me, you will regret it. There's plenty of folks willing to pay top dollar for Mr. Vincente's product. He wanted me to tell you that he's only doing this deal with you in the name of—what did he call it?—international relations. Don't you forget it."

The voice on the other end dropped to a more reasonable volume and Juan smiled. "Mr. Vincente is well aware of the heat. Yeah, yeah, and I checked Weather Channel. Seems like it's just going to get hotter. Mr. Vincente wanted me to remind you of how much riskier this deal becomes the hotter it gets. You'd be smart to keep that in mind in case you're thinking of pulling anything or trying to screw Mr. Vincente. Mr. Vincente doesn't like people trying to screw him, you hear me?"

Juan picked something black from under his fingernail as he listened. Oren looked away when he wiped the gunk on the tabletop. Dani returned with their drinks in time to spot the smear. "Yeah, yeah, Mr. Vincente is well aware of your time issues. We'll do the deal in the morning. We'll discuss the—hang on." He pulled the phone away from his mouth and smiled. "Thanks, Dani. Two cubes, just the way I like it, babe." He slurped a loud drink and went back to the phone.

Oren noticed that even Dani couldn't completely hide her opinion of Juan's ridiculous big-shot gesture. He also didn't miss the way Joaquin managed to brush his fat hand over Dani's left breast reaching for his drink. He really needed to give Dani a raise.

XXX

8:59am, 88° F

Dani wanted a raise. She didn't care about the illegality of whatever deal the Wheelers were putting together. She didn't really even care about Joaquin's clumsy attempts to feel her up. He was big and armed and nasty, but he was also stupid and hungry for attention. Dani didn't have any trouble at all keeping Joaquin in his place. She let him cop his little feels, his greasy thumbs brushing against her here and there. It was like letting steam out of a pipe—little bits here and there kept pressure from building up.

No, Dani wanted a raise for keeping her mouth shut about Caldwell. That wasn't true either. She wanted for Caldwell to never have existed.

She wanted to slap Mr. Randolph on the side of the head with her tray until he truly understood the depths of her hatred for any agent of law enforcement.

Instead, she went back into the bar and fished his laptop out from beneath the cash register. Mr. Randolph never remarked on the fact that someone kept erasing his internet history. Maybe he didn't notice; it wasn't the kind of thing most people paid attention to. Dani did, though. She not only erased hers after every search, she made a point of checking his. Mostly Mr. Randolph checked weather reports and liquor prices; occasionally did a little online shopping for fishing gear. If he did use any search engines, he did it in private browsing or erased his cookies. But judging from the notes he had taped to the machine—*ctrl+alt+delete = 911 shutdown*—he didn't give the impression of being especially tech savvy.

Then again, he didn't need to do any searches himself, did he? He could just call his buddy in the FBI.

Dani glanced around to be sure nobody watched her type. *Char-baneaux.* The name brought up the usual list—the senator, the executives, the charitable foundations. Dani scrolled through the list for anything new. Typing in *Sinclair* and *Choo-Choo* brought up only older entries on gossip sites like Page Six. It seemed her friend and coworker had kept himself out of the gossip sheets after taking the job as audio analyst with Rasmund.

Or Rasmund had removed him from the pages.

Dani didn't feel safe trying to call Choo-Choo on any of the jillion numbers associated with the Charbaneaux name. Nobody had told her contact was forbidden, but she suspected the lurking eyes that tracked her life now wouldn't smile upon fraternization. They might not want two damaged witnesses to the government's covert crimes getting together and swapping stories. She didn't know what lengths they might go to in order to prevent a reunion, but she knew altogether too well what they were capable of.

It didn't keep her from looking for him though.

All of this—all of this running to the Keys and hiding in plain sight, all the Fed shakedowns and intimidations, all the nightmares, especially the nightmares—all of this made her want to talk to the one person on earth who knew what had really happened, who knew she was never a spy or an interrogator or a torturer. She wanted to just sit and be quiet with the one person who wouldn't wonder about the scars on her body because he had scars of his own.

But there was no sign of him. She made note as she always did of any current location for family members. Someone was hosting a gala in New York City next weekend; a Charbaneaux was mentioned in an article about Martha's Vineyard. There was a campaign fundraiser in Philadelphia and a charity auction in San Francisco. Who knew there were so many Charbaneauxs in the world? Dani didn't care about any of them. She wanted only to see her friend Choo-Choo, to make sure he was okay.

She saw Caldwell's glass sweating on the bar.

She smelled Joaquin Wheeler on her clothes.

She wanted Choo-Choo to tell her that she was okay.

CHAPTER FOUR

9:08am, 92° F

Oren tried to be optimistic. The presence (and smell) of Juan and Joaquin Wheeler would do nothing but hurt his business. The upside? He told himself that this time of year and this heat wave would combine to keep his business at a minimum, so losing a day like today wouldn't kill him. He then told himself to avoid any thoughts that included things that would kill him. Wishing he'd brought a napkin so he wouldn't have to make skin contact, he reached for the thick envelope of cash Juan had set between them.

Oren was a practical man. Cash helped.

"Well"—he rose from the chair, willing Juan to do the same—"I guess I'll see you guys tomorrow. Same time? No reason to stick around in this heat."

"I like the heat." Juan didn't rise; he didn't reach for his drink. Oren glanced at Joaquin, who didn't seem to share his brother's enthusiasm for the weather. Joaquin's shirt clung to him, sweat soaked through every inch of it. But Oren knew that until Juan gave the sign, Joaquin would stay put. He was actually glad the tourist season was low.

Then he heard the tinny chimes of "Lady of Spain."

Hoping it was just a sail-by, Oren leaned over the edge of the deck, looking out to the open water. He saw a ratty pontoon boat decorated with Chinese lanterns and enormous plastic parrots puttering into the inlet. Over a dozen people aboard laughed and waved, toasting Oren and Joaquin with plastic margarita glasses as the boat bumped against the dock.

"Fellas, I hate to put you out, but I've got customers." When Joaquin didn't leave his spot at the top of the stairs, Oren looked to Juan. "Would you mind? I have to make a living, and so does Casper."

Juan stared at him for several seconds and Oren began to worry that the sadistic little thug would tell him that Jinky's was officially off-limits for the day. It was exactly the kind of petty power trip the Wheelers were famous for. Instead, Juan shrugged and reached for his drink.

"No problem. There's plenty of free tables. Yo, bro," Juan kicked out a chair beside him and Joaquin hauled himself off the stair railing that he'd been squeezing himself against. "We're just going to hang out here for a while and discuss the arrangements. You do your thing, Randolph, we'll do ours. After all, we're businessmen, aren't we? Professionals, right?"

Oren didn't trust himself to answer convincingly. He turned to wave the guests up.

The captain, Casper van Dosen, tooted the horn. Someone yelled from the far end of the inlet and Oren saw the Australians from Room Six staggering out into the heat, lured by the siren call of the *Lady of Spain*. Like Jinky's, Casper's party boat had a reputation among the neighboring keys and their visitors. The *Lady of Spain* smelled bad, kept an unreliable schedule, and charged far too much for its services. It was also a guaranteed, if not legendary, good time if one could hold one's liquor. Some days it ran sunset cruises; some days it ran sunrise cruises. And on days like today when the open water was just too hot—or

Casper felt like having a plate of fried plantains—the *Lady of Spain* would dock at Jinky's, giving Oren a captive and thirsty audience for the day.

Oren really hoped the morning party crew was already drunk because the way the temperature was rising, the Wheelers would soon smell bad enough to choke on. He headed back into the bar to give Dani a heads-up and get himself the next of what would be many drinks.

X X X

11:20am, 96° F

The third vodka helped the most. Oren felt that hard knot of tension between his shoulder blades give just a fraction. The crowd from Casper's boat settled in around the bar and the surrounding tables, claiming the sun was just too strong. Nobody came out and said it but the presence (and smell) of the two greasy men outside played a part in bringing the party indoors. Oren didn't care where they sat or where they drank as long as they paid. And didn't get shot by the Wheelers. Sometimes you had to take things at their most basic level.

Dani ran the bar with her usual composure. Compared to Peg, she was downright bubbly, but Oren watched her with new eyes. What was it about her that had made Caldwell curious? He hadn't really put much thought into who she might have been before arriving on Redemption Key. Sure, he'd seen the bullet wound and noticed that weird focus with which she did almost everything—running, fixing windows, pouring drinks. It was like she was studying everything. Or maybe it was like she was waiting for everything to explode in her hand. Or like everything was a trick she wasn't going to fall into.

Maybe the fourth vodka was a mistake.

Too late now. Oren sucked on an ice cube and stared over the crowd. The party boat folks clustered near the bar with bandy-legged Casper and his plate of plantains performing like the master of ceremonies.

Angel Jackson showed up at some point, slipping back into the kitchen to meet with Rolly. God only knew what the cook and the black-eyed pilot were up to. An elderly couple who lived down the street from the fish camp strolled in after their morning walk, and another table was filled with guys he hadn't seen come in. Fishermen, probably. The heat did funny things to people in Florida. You just never knew if everyone was going to go to ground or come roaring out for relief.

He watched the Australians try for the millionth time since their arrival to make small talk with Dani. One of them, Nigel or Rigel or something—Oren couldn't make heads or tails out their impenetrable accent—flipped his nasty dreads over his shoulder and pointed to the scar peeking out from below the hem of Dani's dress. Oren chuckled and leaned in to listen; Casper looked up from his plantains. This should be entertaining.

"'S quite a scar you got there," Nigel/Rigel said.

Dani said nothing, just nodded once and garnished a gin and tonic.

Nigel/Rigel said something else unintelligible, and Dani cocked her eyebrow. "Want to try that in English?" she asked.

"I am speaking English," he said, spinning on the stool so his similarly dreaded friends could hear him. "The problem with your culture is you think everyone ought to sound just like you. What you fail to take into account is that the rest of the world would rather hear cats having a naughty than listen to that American shit. You got it all in the nose, you know?"

Dani handed the gin and tonic to Casper, who gave her a wink. She graced him with a friendly flicker of recognition before turning back to the younger man. "Is that what you came all the way from Australia for? To tell me what's wrong with my culture?"

"Nah, came for the good ganja. We're just hoping to get out of here in one piece. You know, not shot to pieces like Butch and Sundance. A sight better than you, eh?"

Dani's face revealed nothing. "What do you mean?"

He nodded toward her leg. "I been around. That there's a gunshot wound. Pretty big one too."

Nigel/Rigel and his friends didn't seem to notice how quiet the bar had gotten during the exchange. "Where did you learn that?" Dani asked. "CSI: Melbourne?"

"Like I said, I been around."

"Not enough, apparently." Dani's eyes flitted over the locals nonchalantly leaning in. "That's not from a bullet." The Australian made a disbelieving sound, and Dani poured herself a shot of tequila. She tilted her head back, telling her tale to the ceiling, which Oren knew made it easier for everyone pretending not to listen to hear her. "I was a pole-vaulter. A good one. Headed to the Olympics. I'd qualified and everything. One day at training, I was up and almost over. The pole snapped, I fell, and the jagged end went right through my leg. Hurt like a son of a bitch. And that was the end of my Olympic dreams."

Casper let out a loud sigh. "Damn shame about the Olympics." He raised his glass to her and Dani toasted him with her shot.

No sooner had the glasses hit the bar than Rolly leaned out the window between the bar and the kitchen and shouted, "Twenty-three!"

"Twenty-three!" the locals shouted back, high-fiving each other as Oren waved his finger in circles over his head. Dani started lining up shot glasses and pouring tequila. That was the twenty-third time someone had asked her about the scar on her leg, and that was the twenty-third original version she had answered with. The locals had never asked and only the stupidest tourists ever did and Oren had promised Casper and friends that for every original answer Dani could create, he'd buy a round for the entire bar. Excluding, of course, the askers, something that sat very badly with the Australians.

Dani slid Oren's fifth vodka before him, the lime squeezed to death exactly the way he liked it. Whatever her story was, there was no denying that Dani Britton fit right in at Jinky's.

XXX

12:15pm, 98° F

Dani climbed out from behind the bar with an empty bucket on her arm and a white bar towel draped over her shoulder, bright against her black knit dress. She stopped by a table of sunburned women and started collecting empty beer bottles, dumping them into the bucket. A breeze caught the hem of the short dress, raising it almost high enough to reveal the scar on her thigh, but Oren noticed she kept the bucket strategically placed. After giving the table a quick pass with her towel, she hoisted the full bucket and headed back to the bar.

"Stop back here after you take care of them," Oren said, and Dani nodded. She delivered a half dozen beers in her bucket for the women who cheered, and came back to Oren.

"Room's ready," she said. "Need it tomorrow?" She banged the empty bucket against her leg, ignoring the water that dripped down onto her red flip-flop.

Oren nodded, sipping his drink. "You turned on the fan, right? I can smell Juan from here. God only knows what they'll smell like by tomorrow." He didn't wait for her to answer, knowing she had taken care of everything. "Crank the AC too. This Bermingham's a Canadian. Word is the farthest south he's come is Miami. I can't imagine he'll be a fan of this heat. You don't know Bermingham, do you? Ever heard of him? No, you wouldn't, would you? You didn't work in Miami, did you? No, you were in Key West, weren't you? Not that you would know someone like him. I mean if Caldwell doesn't know him . . ."

Oren knew he was rambling. The vodka wasn't soothing his nerves but it was certainly loosening his tongue. Dani stood by, swinging her bucket, waiting for him to either dismiss her or ask her a question she could answer.

"It's funny you haven't met Caldwell before today, isn't it? How'd that happen?"

Dani shrugged, scanning the bar to see if anyone needed drinks.

"He says he's seen you around but he hasn't had a chance to meet you. He says you've been ducking him. Have you been ducking him?"

She looked up at him, her pretty, tan face clear and smooth. "Usually when someone tries to get my attention by the units, it's to unstop their toilets or to get a rat out of their room."

She said nothing else, just shrugged as if that explained everything. Oren supposed it did, although couldn't help but think that her excuse sounded an awful lot like an explanation of the bullet wound on her leg.

X X X

Dani felt a dribble of water slide down her right leg where the bucket bumped against her. She loosened her grip on the plastic handle to dry the sweat that coated her palm. If Mr. Randolph was asking about Caldwell, Caldwell had been asking about Dani.

Caldwell and Mr. Randolph were more than just drinking buddies or acquaintances. They trusted each other. That's why Dani had kept her distance from the agent. If Mr. Randolph went to Caldwell for background information on Dani, Caldwell would go to his bosses at the FBI. Who knew what story the powers behind this whole mess would tell about her? It probably wasn't a good one, she would bet. She did bet. She was betting what little shred of normalcy she had carved out here on the generosity of a nameless authority.

Mr. Randolph thought the Wheelers were bad news. The people she had worked for made the psychotic drug dealers look like a Little League team.

The couple at the end needed another round of margaritas, and Dani nodded to them. She could run. She could walk off the deck and climb into the car and be halfway out of the state before sunset.

But where would she go? She had her money, but they had everything else. They had the roads and the law and the cameras and the manpower to find her anywhere she went. They could say anything about her they wanted; they could give her a criminal record and put a warrant out for her arrest. They could make her disappear. They could make jail look like the best-case scenario. They could—

"Damn it, Dani." Mr. Randolph broke her downward spiral of thought. "Is it just me or does Juan look nervous?"

"What? What?" Dani didn't realize she'd been holding her breath.

"Juan Wheeler! Look at him. This deal is bad. I can feel it. I mean, even worse than a regular Wheeler deal." Mr. Randolph gnawed on his lime peel. "Or am I just crazy? Having some kind of midlife crisis?" He arched an eyebrow at her in comic seriousness. "And don't you dare tell me I'm way too old for this to be midlife."

She laughed, relieved to be knocked off her train of thought. "I'll go ask him what cologne he uses. I'll tell him I'm looking for a Christmas gift for you."

Mr. Randolph scrunched up his face in a passable rendition of the smaller Wheeler's scowl, making his eyebrows twitch. "It's the smell of power, *chica*. Power and women. And money. And my mother. Power, women, money, and mother—and not in that order." He let his scratchy falsetto disintegrate into Wheeler's familiar chittering giggle.

Dani laughed again, making a point of not looking at the scowling man out on the deck. Mr. Randolph wasn't checking on her; he wasn't asking Caldwell to. He had a meeting to oversee and a bar to run. He had problems of his own that had nothing to do with her. As far as he was concerned she was just another housekeeper, another bartender. He must have seen her relax because he draped his arm over her shoulder in a paternal hug.

"I'm getting too old for this, Dani. These meetings and these worries." He turned her so they both stared out over the drunken room. "One of these days I'm just going to get on my boat and sail to distant shores. I'll just be gone and this will all be yours. What do you think?"

She knew he had no intention of ever leaving Jinky's. "Do I get to keep Peg and Rolly?"

"Do you have the firepower to get them out?"

He hugged her closer and Dani let herself relax against him. His arm felt warm and heavy on her shoulder. She could have stood there forever. The feeling of solidity, of safety, of belonging, blew in on the hot tidal breeze. Mr. Randolph swayed gently with her, rocking them side by side.

"It's good to have you here, Dani. The customers like you. The locals like you. Hell, even Peg likes you, and she doesn't like anyone."

"She hasn't sprayed me with the hose in months."

"See? You're practically sisters."

She smiled at that, watching as Casper threw a plantain chip into a young woman's mouth. "I like it here, Mr. Randolph."

He nodded. "I'm glad." They stood together in easy silence watching the old captain flirt with his drunken passengers. Finally he patted her arm. "We've got until tomorrow for the meeting. Why don't you run down and tell Peg to help you out up here? Peg needs to burn off some steam, and it doesn't look like anyone's ready to quit drinking. Have Rolly whip you up some conch fritters, okay?"

"Okay, thanks. I'll just do another pass of drinks first." She swung her bucket and ducked back behind the bar. She felt mellow and loose, like she'd just had a good cry or a long nap. Two girls near the deck cooed at a tiny Key deer that strolled out from the bushes below and Dani smiled. She liked it here.

X X X

Oren watched Dani move through the crowd picking up empty glasses and wiping down tables. He'd just given her part of the day off and she still wouldn't stop working. The rental units had never been cleaner and the plumbing hadn't backed up seriously since Dani had taken over maintenance. He'd never had an employee work that hard. He wasn't entirely sure what motivated someone like that.

She took a picture of a couple at the bar, saying something that made them laugh just as the flash went off. Maybe he'd read her wrong earlier. Maybe that smile she'd flashed to Caldwell hadn't been off. Hell, maybe she'd even been flirting with the agent. Stranger things had happened. But Caldwell wouldn't have missed a flirtatious move, even a strange one. He had radar that put the military to shame when it came to reading women, and Caldwell's reaction had been anything but flattered. Oren swirled his ice, a nervous habit he couldn't kick. There couldn't be anything to worry about if his buddy ran a background check, right? What could Dani have done that would be so horrible to unearth?

She pushed past him just then with two margaritas and a bucket of beer. He grabbed her towel and she glanced over her shoulder at him.

"What did I say?" He took the glasses in one hand, the bucket in the other. "You—stop working. Get Peg up here. Drink. Laugh. Shake that little ass you've been running all over hell and back and let Rolly fill you up with some greasy fried food. I own this place, remember? I can serve a drink."

She surrendered the drinks and started pointing out who was expecting what. He leaned down close to her face. "I own this place," he repeated slowly. "Remember?"

"Yes, boss," she said, smiling up at him.

"That's right, I'm the boss. You're the employee. Now sit down and start ripping me off. You're making the rest of the staff look bad."

She giggled at that and headed down to get Peg. More than one man watched the swish of her skirt against her short, tan legs as she headed past them. What could a little thing like that have done that could be so terrible the FBI would have a file?

X X X

99° F

Dani hadn't realized how tense she'd been since meeting Caldwell. A sense of lightness filled her chest. Maybe she hadn't really relaxed since she'd arrived on the island, maybe even since she'd left DC. The sensation left her a little dizzy in a champagne kind of way. That moment with Mr. Randolph, when he'd put his arm around her the way her father used to do, the same soft voice, easy swaying, made her feel safer than she had since her father's death. Dani felt her need to be on Redemption Key, at Jinky's, ache deep inside her, only now the ache didn't feel like fear but like hope.

CHAPTER FIVE

12:40pm, 99° F

Dani knocked on the metal kitchen counter. Rolly whistled into the fan that blew hot greasy air right back at him. "Hey, can I get a scavenge?" Mr. Randolph had told her to eat, but she knew the cook preferred to think the food was a personal favor. A scavenge was when Rolly would pick a piece or two off of several outgoing orders and heap them on a plate for her or Peg. Conch fritters, shrimp, some slices of fried plantain—whatever the crowd was ordering, that's what they got to eat. Dani liked the surprise and she liked the pleased look on Rolly's hangdog face when he would present her with his feast.

"Got one all ready for ya, small fry." He tossed up a plate loaded with fried oysters, grilled shrimp, mango salad, and fried plantains. He scraped a thick wedge of butter on a long slice of cornbread and laid it on top of the food. "You looked hungry. Don't tell Peg I gave you the last of the mango salad. And don't let Casper eat all your plantains!"

Dani laughed, letting the kitchen door swing shut on his orders. With no stools at the bar available, Casper offered to give up his but she waved him off, making the old man smile by jumping up to sit on the bar itself right beside him. He made a show of admiring her legs—without any attention paid to the glimpse of scar that peeked out before she settled—and helped himself to an oyster. Peg slung drinks around her, splashing her with ice and froth, and more than once shouted very near her ear at a waiting customer, but Dani didn't worry about being in the way. If Peg wanted her off the bar, Dani knew she could make that happen.

Casper was entertaining a couple of tourists and she'd come in midway through a story too outlandish to bother catching up with. Instead she laughed and swung her feet, leaning backwards over the bar to make herself a gin and tonic. She ignored the surreptitious glances up the back of her skirt when she reached for the fountain nozzle.

The crowd from the *Lady of Spain* had settled in nicely, happy in their new temporary home. Binge drinkers tended not to enjoy Casper's cruises very much or very long. The people that got the most for their money were those savvy drinkers who could pace themselves to last an hour or an afternoon. There was just no telling how long the captain would stay put in any port. Today looked like it was going to be a long one, and the partygoers seemed up to the challenge.

Dani spied a couple more locals who had drifted in. The heat seemed to be demanding liquor today. Even the old couple, the Emersons, who had the little bungalow down the road, had managed to get up the steps to the bar, Mr. Emerson's walker be damned. Dani scanned the room to see if Angel Jackson had come in. The hard-eyed pilot was the only one Mrs. Emerson would trust to carry her husband down the steps should the Tanqueray get the best of him.

The Texans from Room Five were trying to get Peg's attention, probably to settle their bill and check out, and were having as much luck with that as the Australians were in getting another round of drinks. The fishermen took the delay in stride, settling in at a table against the wall and kicking their feet up like they lived there. Dani thought maybe she should jump down and pitch in, but she saw Mr. Randolph leaning against the bar talking to Angel Jackson like he had all the time in the world. If Mr. Randolph wasn't in a hurry, neither was she.

Casper slapped her thigh at the punch line to some joke she hadn't heard, and the crowd around him cackled. Dani didn't bother to catch the joke, watching instead a thick-muscled man with sandy hair and narrow eyes trying to get Peg's attention. He didn't wave dollar bills around like the Australians, he didn't hold up an empty glass like most of the tourists did. He just leaned on the bar, taking up a lot of space at the crowded rail. Dani sipped her gin and laughed, watching Peg ignore him.

He looked behind him, gesturing to someone she couldn't see about his frustration with the service. With a shrug of surrender he turned back around, watching Peg, hoping to make some kind of eye contact. He must have noticed Dani watching him because he leaned heavily on his forearms and looked up at her.

"Is there a trick to this?"

"Yeah," Dani had to shout over a rash of laughter. "Don't be too thirsty."

"If I had known it would be this hard, I'd have brought my cooler in."

Angel Jackson had slid into the space on the other side of the muscular man and snorted at that. "Glad you didn't, pal. Can't you read?" He pointed to a sign taped to the bar mirror:

Empty coolers will be filled for a price.
Full coolers emptied for free.
Coolers you bring in with beer from outside
Will be chucked to the bottom of the sea.

"Very poetic," he said, shaking his head. "What's her name?"

"What difference does it make?" Angel asked. "She won't answer you."

The sandy-haired man sighed and straightened up. Dani tapped his arm with her foot. "Watch this." She leaned backwards on the bar and shouted, "Hey Peg! I'm eating the last of the mango salad." Dani barely straightened up before an uncut lime went whizzing by her head, smashing into a napkin holder at the far end of the bar. Someone shouted in protest, and Peg answered the complaint with a lemon thrown even harder. Angel turned his back on the flying fruit, leaning against the bar and toasting Dani with his beer.

"See?" Dani nudged the scowling stranger. "It doesn't help to know her name."

"What does help?"

"The trick is," Angel said, "to be here when Dani's behind the bar."

"Dani?" The man leaned back, looking from her to Angel with interest. "And when would that be?"

"That depends." Angel drank the last of his beer and handed the empty bottle over the shorter man's head to Dani. "It depends on who you know."

Dani tossed the empty into the garbage can behind the bar and bent backwards to reach into the cooler for another. She popped the top and smiled, passing the icy bottle slowly past the newcomer's envious gaze. He shook his head as Angel drank, then looked up at her with a smirk.

"You must be Dani."

"I must be."

He studied her face for a moment with a look she couldn't read. A huge hand came down on his shoulder and he didn't jump.

"Come on, Ned, what are you doing? Growing the wheat? Where's the beer?" The man's accent was miles away from Florida—Wisconsin or maybe the Dakotas—but when Dani looked up, the smile she saw was nothing but sunshine. He was tall; even from her perch on the bar she had to look up to see wide brown eyes and deep dimples that were way too cute to be on a grown man's face. He wore his brown hair a touch too long and he stood just a little closer than she usually allowed.

Ned tipped his head toward her. "It seems Dani here is the key."

His eyes widened, his dimples deepening, as he leaned closer into her personal space. As was her way, Dani didn't back off. Only this time it felt less like a challenge, more like an invitation. And she wasn't sure exactly who was inviting whom.

He was night and day from his buddy. Everything about Ned was dense and thick, from the muscles in his neck to the thick, close-cut hair on his head. Where Ned kept his movements small and controlled, Dani saw this man moved with a loping sort of ease and grace. She'd been hit on by a lot of guys since coming to Jinky's. She felt her face warm at the possibility of letting this lanky northerner break her drought. She couldn't even blame the gin. Yet.

"Oh now, you see," Casper interrupted, patting Dani's knee, "Dani here has what we call special dispensation. The rules simply do not apply to her, am I right?" A drunken rumble of agreement rose from the surrounding crowd. The newcomer smiled at Dani as Casper went on. "Which is the very reason why our friends here feel so at home after only just arriving this afternoon on a long journey from Madison, Wisconsin. Isn't that right, Steve? Tony? Chuck?"

"Tucker," he said, winking at Dani. "And this is Ned. We just flew in from St. Paul."

"Exactly," Casper said, raising his glass. "A toast, to Ted and to Michigan!"

"To Michigan!" The crowd roared along. Dani laughed when she saw Tucker raise his empty bottle along with them.

Casper went back to whatever convoluted tale of mayhem he was spinning for his audience, and Tucker somehow managed to get his large frame into a narrow space between the cluster of drunks and Dani's crossed legs. He moved so easily, so comfortably, people just gave way to him. Dani knew that required a certain interpersonal skill that not many people could manage. Tucker made it look easy. Ned surrendered his spot at the bar, letting his friend try his luck at getting them a beer. From the little smile Dani could see on Angel Jackson's profile, the body cues must be pretty clear. Tucker had a much better strategy in place.

"So what is it about you, Dani," Tucker said with a crooked smile, "that gives you the dispensation? That makes you the person who can make these beers magically appear when nobody else can? Do you have some kind of special connection to the owner?"

Dani shrugged, trying not to smile too broadly. Those dimples kept distracting her. "It's not exactly a conspiracy. I work here."

"She works here too," Ned muttered, glaring at Peg, who sat on a cooler ignoring the thirsty patrons down the bar.

"Don't let her hear you complain," Dani warned with mock gravity. "You'll never get a beer. Ever. She has ears like a bat." She twisted backwards once again to dig into the cooler beneath the bar. From the corner of her eye, she could see Ned and Tucker share a glance after checking out her backside. She straightened back up with two Coronas.

Ned huffed. "Don't you have Sam Adams?"

"I can't reach the Sam Adams. Or would you rather wait and ask Peg?"

Tucker took the beers from her, passing one to his scowling friend. "Don't mind Ned. He's just grumpy. Doesn't like the heat."

"I'm thirsty," Ned complained, drinking half the bottle down in one chug.

Tucker didn't drink from his bottle right away. He waited until Dani had settled and handed her her gin and tonic, clinking his bottle against it. "Here's to Dani, and to discovering Jinky's secret weapon."

Two drinks later, Tucker's odds of picking her up were looking better and better and still not because of the gin. Dani paced herself, and either Tucker had great instincts or he was a natural gentleman because he kept his flirtation steady but casual. A few times Dani could feel that old urge to run and hide, to disconnect from anyone who looked too closely at her, but he made a point of keeping Ned and Angel in the circle, letting the passing drinkers and drunks come and go, and keeping Dani from feeling cornered. But he never let her go too long without a private smile.

She was just starting to wonder about the coming evening when Tucker looked up from checking a message on his phone and caught her watching him.

"Business. Yuck." He shoved the phone into his pocket.

"What business are you in?"

He leaned in against the bar, coming the closest to her he had all afternoon. "The kind of business I hope keeps sending me to Florida."

"You don't like Minnesota?"

"Oh you know." He shrugged. "Nine months of winter, three months of bad sledding." He gave a quick glance to the crowd before whispering in her ear. "But I'm a little worried. I've heard the women down here are trouble."

"Is that right?"

"Yeah, real bad news, I've heard. Take you, for example. You seem awfully cute and sweet, but what's going on here?" He flicked his gaze down and quickly back up to her face. "That looks like it might be trouble."

He'd looked at her legs crossed on the edge of the bar. She could feel that the hem of her skirt had ridden up. She didn't want to look to see the edge of the scar he must have noticed.

She'd pulled back slightly when she felt his fingertip trace her thigh. "What's this?" he whispered and she forced herself to look. Her scar was still hidden. His finger was moving through moist splatter on her skin, sliding through tiny orange chunks.

"Oh, that's mango salad. I must have spilled."

When Tucker slipped the tip of his finger between his lips, Dani's breath was part shiver, part giggle. She tried to look worried when Mr. Randolph stomped behind the bar and poured himself another vodka.

"Everything okay, boss?"

He swallowed the drink in one gulp. "For now, yeah. The Wheelers are finally gone. Casper's pulling out in a few, too."

"So do you need me to work tonight?"

He must have heard the hopeful tone in her voice or noticed Tucker's hand on her thigh. "Sure, take the night off. Hell, we could all be dead tomorrow."

Dani grinned at Tucker.

Then Angel Jackson shouted to someone down the bar and threw a wrench in Dani's plans. Tucker's hand was warm on her thigh and those dimples were really cute, but Angel Jackson was making an up-and-back flight tonight to Boston. That was close to one of the locations on her list. She waved the black-eyed pilot over.

"Any chance you could drop me at Martha's Vineyard?"

"Drop you there?" Angel asked, ignoring Tucker. "Got a parachute?"

"No, but I've got something to do there."

He laughed and emptied his beer. "Not running a taxi service, kid."

"You told me you owed me one after that Ohio deal."

Tucker leaned back from the conversation but Dani knew he still listened. She didn't want to give too many details about Angel's business but she didn't want to miss this chance. Of all the places she'd seen the Charbaneauxs mentioned, Martha's Vineyard was the most likely place to find Choo-Choo. He'd told her he'd probably wind up there. If she flew there commercially, she had no doubt her name would ping security. It would take forever to drive there, and even if she did, the tracker in her car would let whoever watched her know where she was headed. With a private jet, she could get in and get out with nobody knowing she was trying to reach her friend.

Dani put a lot of faith in her paranoia.

She also knew just how pissed the pilot had been when that kid from Ohio tried to rip him off. Angel Jackson was nobody to screw with. He stared at her with hard eyes as black as the braid that ran down his back, but she didn't blink.

"You know it's like seven hours each way. Gotta stop to refuel."

"I can give you money for gas."

He snickered. "That's all been taken care of by my client. That's not the point."

"What is the point?"

He seemed to think about that. "It's out of my way."

"Not by much. I've looked at maps."

"It's an up-and-back. You'd only have about two hours; three, tops."

"Okay." She did some quick math. She'd be lucky to have until midnight to find her friend. Still, it was better than her odds of him strolling into the bar to find her. She saw the moment Angel relented, his shoulders settling.

"Okay then. I'll take you on one condition. Tell me how you knew those bundles of cash were fake."

Dani smiled. "The kid kept scratching his hand where the ink stains were. A lot of people are allergic to newspaper ink. Plus he had three rubber bands around his wrist."

Angel stared at her. "You're shitting me. You called out some dude based on rubber bands and an itchy hand?"

She kept smiling. Of course it had been more than that. Years of watching surveillance tapes of people engaging in corporate espionage, to say nothing of a childhood spent roaming the country with her trucker father, had given Dani an eye for tells. The Ohioan had all but hung a sign around his neck saying, "Don't look at the money!" Still, Dani didn't see any reason to spill all her secrets. A little mystery was a powerful thing.

It was getting her to Martha's Vineyard.

She hopped off the bar to tell Mr. Randolph she'd be leaving. He said fine, so long as she was back to work his meeting in the morning. Plus she wanted to put sneakers on. It might sound dumb, but Dani didn't want to find herself somewhere she didn't know without at least having the ability to run with ease. She debated packing a weapon, maybe just the small shank she'd honed. It was Martha's Vineyard after all, not Detroit. Still, DC had been a pretty civilized city and she sure wished she'd had a blade there. In a private plane there wouldn't be any airport security, right?

A large hand on her arm jolted her from her thoughts. Tucker tilted his head at her, his eyes wide, his confusion showing in his smile.

"You're leaving?"

"Oh. Yeah. I have to . . ." It occurred to her then that her habit of shuttling off thoughts when a more important one came along probably didn't make her the most socially adept person. In one conversation she had completely dismissed Tucker from her thoughts. That probably wasn't normal. Of course, it also wasn't normal—her normal, at least—for anyone to question her comings and goings. Especially her goings. And especially guys who looked like Tucker.

"Let me guess." He studied her with mock seriousness, those damn dimples drawing her in. "This isn't the only place you're indispensible. Bars everywhere call to you when lonely tourists can't get their drinks."

She nodded. "It's kind of my superpower."

"Are you coming back?"

The question felt serious and Dani surprised herself by blushing. "I hope so. But I've never flown with Angel before."

He stared at her long enough that getting nervous became an option. Then he winked. "Good. Maybe I'll still be here. If you're lucky. Are you lucky, Dani?"

"No," she said with a laugh. She pushed past him and called over her shoulder. "But I'm smart, and that's better."

CHAPTER SIX

Murfreesboro, TN
1:10pm, 82° F

"You see, it's really just one chain that you loop back onto itself. You do that over and over with alternating rows, and before you know it, you have a peony!"

"Isn't that clever?" Booker turned the fluffy pink bundle of yarn over in his fingers, examining the stitching. "And then, what? You sew it onto a hat or a scarf?"

Mrs. Beverly turned the flower over, showing him where the stitches came together. "It's called appliqué, and you can put it on a hat or a scarf or even on baby blankets and afghans. My granddaughter made the most darling bed throw using different types of flowers appliquéd to a pale green throw. It looked just darling."

"Oh, I don't know if I'll ever reach that level. I'm a rank beginner." He crossed his legs, pulling the skein of yellow yarn closer to him. "That's why I stopped by here today, hoping to pick up a few tips."

Mrs. Beverly patted him with a veiny hand, her milky eye winking girlishly at him. "You're doing just fine, Tom. Just fine. I think it's just wonderful that you stopped in here with us today for our class."

"Here" was the Linebaugh Public Library in Murfreesboro, Tennessee, and the class was a free workshop called Hooks and Gabbers, a crochet class and discussion group, complete with sweet tea and wedding cookies.

Booker checked his stitches. He'd finally found the right shade of yellow he'd been looking for, the same yellow of a certain duvet cover he so vividly remembered snuggling up under all those months ago. An afghan wouldn't be quite as good, but really, what would?

The crochet had been part of his physical therapy. What a surprise that had been—waking up chained to a bed, breathing tubes down his throat, his head screwed in place with a monstrous halo, his face numb and bandaged. They told him he'd been lucky. He hadn't felt very lucky, but looking back he realized they were right.

When Dani had thrown herself over that railing into the blackness of the Tidal Basin—and how many of his dreams had featured that unbelievable sight?—she'd slammed his head down against the metal fence, shattering his cheekbone, nearly blinding him, and giving him a whopper of a concussion. The doctors told him that that damage is what saved his life, that going unconscious kept him from moving. If he had been leaning just another inch or two forward, his neck would have taken the weight of Dani's fall. That damned pouch would have snapped his neck, if not ripped his head clean off. As it was, he suffered severe esophageal trauma, dislocated neck vertebrae, and he had to have the left side of his face reconstructed.

They'd done an amazing job.

Once the bandages came off and the swelling went down, Booker saw no signs of the incisions. They'd gone in through his nose, and he was happy to see his eyes looked the same, his mouth eventually moved the way it was supposed to, and the headaches came less and less frequently. The biggest problem had been pinched nerves and stiffness in his shoulders and arms. That's where the crochet came in, to rebuild fine motor skills.

Well, that and to help him pass the psych evals.

He'd expected more interrogations. He knew he'd missed quite a bit of them, zonked out on the endless painkillers running through his bloodstream. He'd told them about the money, some of it at least, because as soon as they released him, he checked, and three of his five accounts had been emptied. Figured. It always came back to money with these people.

He remembered coming up from one hazy dream world and telling the guard that the only presidents they really protected were the dead ones.

Booker chuckled and Mrs. Beverly smiled at him. "Did I say something funny?"

"Oh, just woolgathering." He held up his fingers draped in yarn. "So to speak!"

The old woman's laugh sounded just like a little bell, and Booker could feel her bony shoulder brush against his arm more than was absolutely necessary. The other women in the group snuck glances at him and threw looks to Mrs. Beverly that ranged from amused to covetous to downright scandalized. Let them stare, he thought. He liked the high color on the old woman's mottled cheeks, the way she clasped her hands together in delight and rocked forward to catch his every word. If Booker's friendly flirtation made her day, it did the same for him.

Plus she possessed extraordinary crochet skills.

He'd still been confined to bed, trying to learn to make daisy chains, when the inevitable meeting began. The woman in the navy blue suit, iron-jawed, shellacked hair, with two gravel-chewing thick-necks in tow. Mentions of dossiers and skill sets and threats disguised as promises. He'd known it was coming. They knew who he was and what he did and they wanted him to work for them.

He hated them for it.

Not enough to turn them down but he hated them for it.

So now he sat in the sunny public library flirting with Mrs. Beverly and learning to make those adorable yarn peonies, killing time after taking out an overweight building contractor this morning for no reason Booker cared to know.

"Are you making that afghan for anyone in particular?"

Booker smiled. He'd been drifting, ignoring Mrs. Beverly. He couldn't have that. Spreading the growing yellow blanket out over his knees, he sighed. "This is for the most precious girl in the world. My little Dani." Several women cooed at that. "I haven't gotten to see her for a while, and I'd really like to have something special for her."

Mrs. Beverly clucked. "Divorce is so difficult for families. The separation . . ."

He nodded, twisting the yarn into another chain stitch. "It is indeed but it's my obligation to keep the relationship intact. It's up to me to let my little Dani know that I'm thinking about her and there is nothing in this world that's going to keep me from seeing her again."

Mrs. Beverly refreshed his tea.

X X X

Martha's Vineyard, MA
9:50pm, 72° F

Dani didn't know an island could have so many trees. Not palm trees, either. From the plane they had looked like regular pine trees but down on the ground, she saw that many of them grew twisted and gnarled, their scabby trunks jutting out at odd angles. Maybe it was because the sun had already set, throwing weird shadows through the forests, but Dani's initial impression of Martha's Vineyard was a creepy one.

The Google search had mentioned a Charbaneaux on Martha's Vineyard—Maisey Charbaneaux-Fulks, helping organize something called MenemShenanigans. Jackson told her that Menemsha was a town on the island. Dani didn't care why these shenanigans would be taking place in a different town, called Chilmark. She didn't care about Maisey Charbaneaux-Fulks or the money they were raising for an art colony on an island that looked like it contained more than its share of the world's wealth. What she cared about was finding Choo-Choo, seeing him for herself, making sure he was okay.

The last time she'd talked with him, she'd been afraid he would kill himself.

After Rasmund, Dani hadn't lost everything. She had the freedom to reinvent herself. She had no close family, nobody expecting anything from her. Choo-Choo had been ordered to be the Prodigal Son, returning repentant to his disapproving family. The look on his face when he'd told her their plan to cover up the true story of the Rasmund incident still haunted Dani. So she'd just flown a thousand miles up the East Coast to an island she knew nothing about to crash a party she wasn't invited to in order to find a woman somehow related to Choo-Choo to ask if he was okay.

If the Feds had a problem with that, they could go fuck themselves.

Jackson had been right about getting around the island. Even at night, she'd been able to hitch a ride in no time. A golden-tanned family with a matching Golden Lab didn't hesitate to let her climb into their Jeep. They'd heard about the party she mentioned, and Dani could hear a distant twinge of disappointment that they hadn't been invited and didn't know exactly where it was. Instead they dropped her at a little market that looked like it had been airlifted from the Deep South circa 1950, charmingly rustic with bins of fruits and vegetables on the porch, and several old bikes with woven baskets leaning unlocked against the railing.

The illusion took a hit when Dani saw the shelves stocked with fourteen dollar jars of English lemon curd, exotic tapenades, and wines she couldn't pronounce. She ventured to the high wooden counter in the back and found a straight-backed old woman with enough New England crust to be an extra on *Murder, She Wrote.*

"Of course there are Charbaneauxs on the Vineyard. Always have been. If you want to find them tonight you've come to the right place. That way." She pointed to her left.

"Could you be a little less specific?" Dani deadpanned.

"I could, but that wouldn't be very neighborly. Keep walking that way. You'll hear the music. It's a wonderful celebration." Her smile could have been sarcastic, or maybe the mirth had been worn away by the years. "Too bad you're here at the end of it."

"I'll make a note for next year."

Dani's mood soured as she hiked the narrow roads winding through the darkness in the general direction the old woman had pointed. The houses, if they could be called that, got larger and farther off the road the longer she walked, but she could hear music rolling toward her so she figured she had to be close. Of course *close* didn't really count when none of the roads she ventured onto led to anything but more roads and fewer houses, the last of the sunlight vanishing behind the scrubby pines.

She berated herself for the stupidity of this plan. She was going to wind up lost on a tiny island. When something rustled in the shadows of the biggest rhododendron bushes she had ever seen, she started berating herself for not checking to see if Martha's Vineyard had any wolves or wildcats protected in its well-preserved bosom. She had just decided to turn around and try to find her way back to the little market when a Range Rover roared around the bend, illuminating the road ahead—a road lined as far as the eye could see with matching Range Rovers. That was a very good sign.

By the time Dani made it up the winding drive she was glad she'd taken up running. Despite what she'd seen on the map, this didn't feel like a small island. The house—again, an understatement—sprawled across a wide, sloping expanse, porches layered three and four levels deep toward what smelled like water in the distance. Lanterns hung everywhere, casting warm shadows over a crowd that danced and drank and laughed. African drum music kept bodies swaying around waiters laden with trays of something that smelled delicious.

Dani had chosen to live in Florida because she thought it was as far from her Oklahoma childhood lifestyle as she could get. She had been wrong. This house, this island, felt like another planet to her.

Planet Choo-Choo.

She didn't spy anyone as beautiful as her friend, but as a whole, the crowd possessed that same long-limbed elegance, that ownership of the air around them that had always set Choo-Choo apart from the simply fine-looking. This wasn't the sleek fashion and glittering jewelry of Miami; the colors were muted, the fabrics stylishly rumpled, and the accessories the women sported seemed more like hardware than fine jewelry.

But the people were gracious. They smiled when she said Charbaneaux; they hid most of their surprise when she asked about Choo-Choo. Everyone seemed to know him, or of him, and a few thought they'd seen him at the party. They shared meaningful glances when they thought she wasn't looking. Passing deeper into the party, through a colossal patio room to yet another array of porches full of lanterns and food and partygoers, Dani sensed she was getting close. The reactions to Choo-Choo's name became more guarded, the eyebrows arched higher, and more than one person let their gaze drift to a section of porch screened behind a trellis of grapes.

She headed into the shadows of the trellis, the music growing fainter behind her, the crowd thinning out to nothing. The only light on this corner of the house came from a red Moroccan lantern hanging off the eave. It took a moment to make out the shape in the darkness.

Choo-Choo sprawled in a deep Adirondack chair. His blond hair caught the red glow and the sliver of his profile was expressionless.

Dani had seen a man sitting like this before, sprawled in a chair, face expressionless. That had been at Rasmund. He had been shot in the head. That's when her world had fallen apart.

It couldn't be happening again.

No, something moved. She thought he had shifted but as she regained her nerve and stepped closer, she saw that Choo-Choo wasn't alone. Someone kneeled between his thighs, a blond French braid visible as it rose and fell in a steady rhythm.

Oh.

She must have said that out loud because Choo-Choo turned his head, finding her in the shadows. His expression didn't change.

"What are you doing here?"

Dani didn't know where to look as the blond girl between his legs lifted her head and wiped her lips. "What do you think I'm doing?" the girl asked, annoyed. "How much have you had to drink tonight?"

"I'm not talking to you." He nudged her with his knee and ignored her grunt of protest, staring at Dani. "What are you doing here?"

"I've been looking for you," Dani managed to say. The girl spun at the sound of her voice.

"Get out of here," he said.

"What?" Dani and the girl spoke in unison.

"Not you," Choo-Choo said to Dani and then nudged the girl again. "Get out of here." He sat straighter in the chair and the girl tumbled backwards. He ignored the long string of profanity that poured out of her mouth, an unrelated string of *fuck* and *prick* and *shithead* jumbled together and trailing behind her as she ran back toward the party. Dani tried not to look too closely as he tucked himself back into his loose linen pants.

"You're really hard to find," she said.

"Am I? I wouldn't think so."

Dani stepped closer, not knowing what to do with her hands or how to stand. Of all the scenarios she'd pictured, this cold reception wasn't one of them. Choo-Choo sat in the only chair on the porch, forcing her to stand like a student called to the principal's office.

He let her stand there for several moments before he spoke. "Did you know there is not one single Danielle Britton in the entire state of Oklahoma? Not one. It's not that unusual a name, is it? What do you suppose the odds of that are? And I had it on excellent authority there would be at least one." He shrugged, the closest thing to an expression he'd shown so far. "I didn't look any further than Oklahoma. I figured you had your reasons to lie to me."

"I didn't lie to you." She took a step closer, trying to read him. "I lied to them."

"Of course, because that would keep 'them' from finding you."

"I didn't know where I was going. They were recording everything we said. They dumped me on the sidewalk with just my car keys. I just—"

"What the fuck, Choo-Choo?" A tall, bronzed woman stomped onto the porch, her armload of thick copper cuffs clanking together. She stopped when she saw Dani. "Who are you?" The woman didn't wait for her answer. "What the fuck? I mean seriously. Sibbie is in tears telling everyone that you hit her. Did you hit her?" He didn't react. "Jesus Christ, Choo-Choo. I don't know why I let you in the door. I really don't. I don't need your scene. I don't need this shit. If you can't behave like a human being why don't you and your . . . your . . ." she waved her hand in Dani's direction, "get the fuck out of my house."

Choo-Choo sighed. "Fuck off, Caroline."

"Fuck you!"

Dani said nothing. She thought she had a filthy mouth, but from what she'd seen tonight, these people tossed f-bombs like confetti. She wondered if they even heard the word anymore.

Caroline studied Dani once more. "I don't know who you are or what the fuck you're doing here, but hopefully you have enough sense to avoid this blond hot-mess piece of shit. Take my advice. He doesn't pay off."

Choo-Choo gave a halfhearted eye roll as she stomped back off the porch, returning to the party. He let the silence grow awkward again before he spoke. "How long are you here?"

"I'm flying out at midnight. That airport in the middle of the island."

He rose from the chair with the same feline grace she remembered. He didn't look at her. "Congratulations on finding me. Have a safe trip back to wherever it is you call home."

"Wait."

His smile was tight. "If you'll excuse me, I must go and make peace with the tribe. After all, these are my people, aren't they? It won't do to let hard feelings fester."

He breezed past the trellis toward the party.

Just like that, Dani stood alone in the dark. Choo-Choo was gone.

XXX

Dani found her own cache of profanity as she made her way through the darkness back to the main road. She'd come all this way for nothing. She'd hoped, no she'd *expected* him to have missed her as much as she'd missed him. It was stupid. She was stupid. They hadn't been close friends at Rasmund. None of them had been the close-friend type.

But after everything that had happened . . .

He'd taken a bullet for her. She remembered two shots ringing out, his long body falling over hers to push her out of danger. Was she remembering it right? Maybe he'd just been ducking for cover. Maybe she'd just imagined their closeness after the grueling ordeal of recovery. Maybe she had made up a bond that never existed.

He thought she'd lied to him.

"Fuck!" Dani shouted to nothing. They'd been monitored in the military hospital. Every word was recorded. She just wanted to get away from them, and Choo-Choo was nowhere near ready to be released. He needed weeks of recuperation.

Because he'd taken that bullet in the chest.

And he thought she'd lied to him.

She grappled with the idea of going back in and forcing him to listen to her, to let her explain. But she'd seen him in the crowd as she left, his arm draped around the mollified Caroline, a cluster of people laughing at whatever was falling from his beautiful mouth. He was home. He was in his element. However he might have felt about it during his years at Rasmund, he had obviously come to accept his place in his world.

Dani decided she hated Martha's Vineyard. It was dark. Not dark like the remote Redemption Key. There were no streetlights on purpose. Only money, real money, could buy this kind of maintained rustic charm. What kind of island didn't have houses with beach towels hanging from the railings? Where were the aboveground pools and plastic floaties? What the hell was lemon curd and why did it cost fourteen dollars a jar?

The best thing about her inner tantrum was that it made the miles pass beneath her feet as she stomped along, hoping she was headed toward the airport. She cleared a small bend in the road and saw a figure leaning against a rough wooden fence.

"Taking the long way?" Choo-Choo asked.

Dani looked around her, trying to find the road he must have taken to beat her here. "I don't even know if I'm going the right way."

He stuck out his thumb and headlights magically appeared. A busted-up, blue-and-white Range Rover pulled over, and Dani heard the strains of bluegrass music pouring from the window. He opened the door for her, letting her crowd in with the pack of twenty-somethings who greeted them with way too much enthusiasm, in

Dani's opinion. She did catch the hiccup of attention when at least two of the passengers recognized Choo-Choo.

"West Tis," he said, slamming the door. Dani knew he felt it too.

"I didn't lie to you," she said softly as they pulled back out onto the road.

"I know." He rolled an unlit cigarette between his fingers, then motioned for her to wait.

She sat close enough beside him that their thighs touched. He didn't pull away. His shirt was open several buttons and she could see the edges of a jagged scar.

They said nothing as they rode, listening to a heated argument about the set list at some Avett Brothers concert and pretending they didn't see the surreptitious glances at Choo-Choo. When they pulled up to the front of the small airport, Choo-Choo didn't even wait until they'd stopped before opening the door. No thank-you, no good-bye, he just stepped down from the car and waited for Dani. She could hear the laughter as they pulled away.

They sat side by side on an outdoor bench, watching small planes and private jets taxi here and there. Martha's Vineyard airport was a busy place for the rich at midnight.

Dani's fingers were soft. He didn't flinch when she pulled down the collar of his shirt to look. She saw that he would have to take it off for her to see the entire scar.

"When did you get out?"

"Three months ago."

"What?" That was nearly twice as long as she'd been held.

Choo-Choo made a sound that tried to be a laugh. "There were complications." Dani waited while he rolled the unlit cigarette back and forth in his hand. The muscles in his jaw clenched and tightened, and it looked like his mouth struggled to either form words or keep them in. He stared straight ahead as he spoke.

"Their story needed some amending."

68

Dani remembered the story. "The alleged party yacht in the Seychelles."

He nodded. "It didn't quite cover the presence of an enormous bullet hole in my chest. If you can believe it, they had me say that we had been attacked by pirates." Dani would have laughed at that if his lips didn't look so tense. "It seemed a bit lurid to me, but everyone bought it. Everyone except Grandfather."

"Your grandfather didn't believe you fought pirates?"

"Grandfather didn't believe any of it. He didn't believe I'd walked away from Rasmund. He started asking questions right away, hiring his own people." He turned to stare at her, his eyes cold. "You can imagine how well that sat with our employers. So they had to *sell* the story."

Dani tried not to show her relief when he dragged his gaze away from her. Choo-Choo was still so beautiful—his high cheekbones, his perfect nose, his now sun-kissed skin. But there was something off about him, something hard and scary under his beauty. Something sad.

He licked his lips several times, his mouth sounding dry as he spoke. "They gave me this . . . creation. A chemical cocktail, something custom-made." His eyes fluttered shut and his voice grew breathy. "It was magical. It was magic. It shimmered underneath my skin like angels. It was heaven on fire. It was . . . it was the love of my life."

His lips parted, his eyes stayed closed.

"Then they took it away."

He drew back into himself, swallowing hard. "They gave me a few days to truly appreciate the depth of my loss before they bundled me up and deposited me in a men's room in Penn Station. Fun fact: writhing on the floor, biting on the metal door frame while shitting yourself will not get you thrown out of a men's room in Penn Station."

"Oh Choo-Choo . . ."

"I think it took two days for my family to find me. Nobody asked me any questions after that. Clearly the pirate story had been a little fantasy I'd spun for them. The 'real' story was as convincing as they'd figured it would be. Junkies *will* get shot from time to time, after all."

Dani didn't know what to say. She watched him turn the cigarette end over end. "Are you clean now?"

He laughed. "As a whistle. You could give my blood to a Girl Scout."

"Well that's good, right?" She rubbed her hand along his leg. "You've kicked it."

He caught her wrist and squeezed hard enough to make her wince. His voice was a hiss. "I haven't kicked shit. I would do anything—anything—for one taste. I would sell my eyes. I would peel off every inch of my skin and crawl over salted razor blades for one drop. Nothing compares to it. Smack, crack, oxy—nothing comes close. I've tried. It's like jumping off a stepladder to reach the moon. I can't even kill myself because I'm afraid I'll miss a chance to feel that one more time. There isn't anything that comes close. So I don't do anything."

He dropped her arm and stared straight ahead. "I don't do anything but want. I want and I want and I want. And I hate."

CHAPTER SEVEN

Murfreesboro, TN
9:50pm, 82° F

"You have got to be kidding me!"

The secure phone he had been given by his handler chirped again. Two jobs in one state? In one day? Booker figured if he had done this many jobs on his own before being compromised by the US government, he could have retired five years ago. As it was, he worked twice as hard now for a tenth of the money and it was really starting to annoy him.

Did they not have anyone else they could call?

Booker had never minded killing people. It didn't thrill him; it didn't repel him. He was never haunted by any of his victims. Except his first one, and she haunted him for reasons other than the bloody mess he'd left her in over twenty years ago.

Almost thirty years ago.

God, he was getting old.

This job, this new "arrangement," wasn't helping things. Thanks to the broad reach of his new employer, Booker had clocked more air miles this year than ever and Booker hated airports. He could feel his soul wearing thinner and thinner with every pat-down, every inane TSA checkpoint. And because his employer was also the employer of every TSA agent in America, his documents and identity passed inspection without a second glance.

It was boring.

Booker scrolled through the message on the screen, reading the details of the next target, and started to laugh. Unbelievable. No, completely believable. And predictable. He had known it was just a matter of time.

Booker typed in his obligatory assent—like he could say no—and his smile widened. This could work out very well for him. The doctors had been right. Booker was lucky.

X X X

11:35pm, 77° F

"I thought you'd be scarier looking."

"I get that a lot."

"Where's your piece?"

Booker sighed, reaching for the plastic tote bag in the floor well between his feet. "I've got everything I need."

Agent Gregory Davis took another bite of his shawarma, ignoring a dribble of greasy white sauce that fell on his suit. The car they were parked in stunk of garlic and onion and the stinging smell of the athletic cream the federal agent wore. Davis's sunburn made his pale red hair paler. When he'd picked Booker up at the hotel, the agent had tried to regale him with tales of the weekend softball game where he'd gotten the burn and the pulled shoulder muscles. Booker had shut the conversation down with an icy stare. Judging from the stuttered mid-sentence halt, Booker figured the agent found him scary enough.

"So you're some kind of consultant, right?"

"Something like that." Booker felt around in the tote.

"Not FBI though. So what? NSA?" Booker said nothing and Davis nodded, talking around another greasy bite. "You're some kind of interrogation specialist. You're going to get our suspect to talk, right? What do you use? Brass knuckles? Drugs? Because, hey buddy, this gangbanger eats guys twice your size for lunch. What is that?"

"An afghan."

"An afghan?" He spit a piece of lettuce onto the seat near Booker's leg. "You're gonna knit while we're on stakeout?"

"It's crochet and it's very relaxing."

"Yeah I bet. What are you making next? Your prom gown?"

Booker began another row, pulling several lengths of yarn free of the bag. "May I ask you a question?"

"It's about time. I'm getting pretty tired of the sound of my own voice."

"Me too." Booker didn't wait for the agent to catch the insult. "Your laptop. Does that have access to FBI files?"

Davis slowed down his chewing to squint at him. "I can login. Why?"

"Would you? I'd like you to look up someone for me."

"Why? Why can't you do it? You're such a hotshot."

"It's complicated." Booker looked up at the scowling redhead. As expected, the agent looked away. Not many people would stare him down. "You should understand that."

"What the hell does that mean?"

"Finish your sandwich." He handed him a napkin. "I don't want you to spit it out all over me when I tell you what comes next."

Davis had sense enough to do as ordered. Booker had turned forty-one in the hospital; the agent had to be almost a decade younger. The redhead also had four or five inches and at least forty pounds on him but still had the instincts to sense a threat.

Being corrupt often gave people that sense.

Booker nodded toward the backseat and Davis reached back for his laptop. He opened the machine and brought it to life but paused at the FBI login screen.

"Start talking."

Booker finished the row he'd been working on and flipped the yellow afghan over on his knees. "You think I'm here to help you interrogate your suspect, right? I don't even know who your suspect is."

"What are you here for?"

"Login."

"Talk first."

Booker stared squarely into the agent's red face. After a second or two, Davis reddened further and typed in his password. Booker went back to his crochet. He didn't know what it was about his stare that so unnerved people and he didn't care. It worked.

"They're onto you," he said to the man. "The Bureau . . ." The agent's fingers froze on the keyboard. "They know you've been selling information, and they know your backup plan is to blackmail your supervisor with some damaging sexual misconduct allegations. Your supervisor is a well-connected man. You should have picked a better target. They know you can prove he's guilty and they know there is no way to keep that information private if you come forward with the evidence."

Davis shook his head. "And they sent you to scare me into giving up the evidence."

"No," Booker said. "They sent me to kill you."

Davis sputtered. "That's . . . no, you're full of shit. You're trying to trap me into admitting something. You're wearing a wire, right? Well I got shit to say to you. I'm not dirty and if you—"

"You are dirty. They've found your money trail. What they can't find is your evidence. Their thinking is: I kill you, the information leak stops, and the evidence against your supervisor dies with you.

They blame your death on your gangbanger and take him down as a bonus prize. Very tidy."

Davis watched Booker's fingers move over the yarn. "Why are you telling me this?"

"Because we are in a unique position to help each other. I'm not supposed to access a particular file that you can access. You're not supposed to walk away from this encounter. You help me; I help you."

Booker didn't flinch when the muzzle of Davis's gun pressed against his temple. He did notice with some happiness that the residual numbness from his surgeries was abating.

"What if I just blow you away right now, blame the banger, and take the credit?"

"Because the people you work for sent me. Trust me. People like this have backup plans you wouldn't believe. If I don't call in within the hour, they activate your tracker and will hunt you down within two hours for killing another federal agent."

"What tracker?"

Booker flicked the damp lettuce shred off the seat. "The tracker you swallowed. How was your shawarma?" Davis swallowed loudly. "I'm looking for a woman."

"How are you supposed to do it? To kill me?"

"The next time you turn the key, the ignition sets off enough C-4 to vaporize the car. I'm told it's the signature move of your suspect."

The gun drifted as the agent thought, then snapped back up against Booker's skull. "Bull. Shit. This is my car. I picked you up. Nobody had access to it."

"It's an easy bomb to rig. Only takes a few seconds if you know what you're doing. So I'll ask you again, how was your shawarma?"

Booker could see the agent struggling to re-create the timeline, trying to gauge how long he'd been out of the car to run to the corner stand for his food. Booker gave him all the time he needed, although he thought the process took an embarrassing length of time.

"But if the car blows," Davis at last came out with, "you blow with it. And if you try to get out of the car, I'll blow you away." He pulled the trigger back.

Booker pulled several more lengths of yarn free of the tote. "I'll just wait for the tranquilizer to kick in." He held up a hand to stop Davis from speaking. "Please don't ask, 'What tranquilizer?' Do I really need to ask you about the shawarma again?"

Davis dropped the gun on top of the keyboard in his lap. Booker let him think his thoughts and weigh his options, listening as the agent's breath grew more ragged. "How is this going to work?"

"You have been targeted for a government-sanctioned execution. One thing these people do better than orchestrate hits is arrange unbreakable alibis. Essentially you are invisible right now. Nobody is watching your file; nobody is tracking your case. Everyone who could be implicated is busy-busy-busy doing anything other than interacting with you. That means that for the next hour, nobody will check to see what you're doing in the FBI database. You can find the woman I'm looking for. If you do, I let you walk. I tell them you overpowered me and you got away."

"But the tranquilizer. The tracker."

"I've got an amphetamine in my bag that will counteract the drug. It's laboratory-grade speed that will have the added bonus of making you shit out the tracker, assuming that disgusting shawarma doesn't do it first. I assume you have some sort of getaway plan already in place."

"Yeah, yeah." Davis nodded rapidly. "I do. It's a good one. Solid. Okay, yeah. Okay. What's the name you're looking for?"

"Danielle Kathleen Britton." He spelled the last name.

"There's no file on her." He scanned through screens as Booker wrapped up the afghan and zipped it into the plastic tote. "She's not in here."

"She's in there. She's somewhere."

"Nothing active. At least nothing I have access to."

"Don't you have some sort of people-finding capabilities at your disposal? You are the Federal Bureau of Investigation."

Davis scowled at him. "It's nothing a private eye couldn't do for you."

"Consider yourself hired. Unless you'd rather I just kill you."

The redhead swore and began typing. "Here. There's a Danielle Kathleen Britton employed at someplace called Jinky's Fish Camp on Redemption Key in Florida. What the hell?" He laughed. "You looking for a little tail with your tail?"

Booker stared at him. "What does that even mean?"

"You know, the fish, like . . . fish tails with, you know, the piece of ass . . ."

The words died on his lips as Booker leaned over the seat to see the face he'd been waiting all these months to see. The picture was so much like her Rasmund identification card. He bit his lip as he took in the messy black hair and little white smile. "She's very special." He smiled up at Davis. "I bet she tans really well. I bet she looks adorable with a tan."

Davis nodded, unconvinced. "You got what you need? We good?"

"Redemption Key. Sounds intriguing, doesn't it?"

"Hey, buddy, are we good?"

Booker grinned. "Oh yeah. We're good. I really appreciate you helping me with this."

Before Davis could thank him for saving his life, Booker jammed the crochet hook through the agent's right eye, then gripped the back of the stunned man's skull and slammed his face against the steering wheel.

"And this is for the tail comment."

A quick jerk to his jaw and the agent's neck snapped cleanly.

Booker wiped his hands on the shawarma-stained napkins.

XXX

Jinky's, FL
Thursday, August 22
7:25am, 86° F

Oren didn't know why Dani had wanted to fly up with Jackson to Boston. He figured she had her reasons. He could admit he didn't know Dani that well, but in a million years he never would have thought she'd come back from anywhere with the guy she strolled back into Jinky's with. He looked like he'd stepped off the pages of some snotty French catalog for the Beautiful People. His floppy blond hair and girl-pretty face made Oren itch to rough him up, and it had been years since Oren's roughing-up days.

Dani was a cute girl, but this guy? Guys like that didn't waste time with girls like Dani, if they wasted time with girls at all. The kid moved with all the bored disdain of a cat as he climbed onto the barstool, waiting while Dani straightened out her schedule with Peg. What kind of hold did he have over Dani? What on earth could those two possibly have in common?

The kid leaned forward, the collar of the loose white shirt sliding down. Oren saw the edge of what looked like a massive set of scars.

They looked a lot like Dani's scars.

Oh.

XXX

7:33am, 86° F

"Whoa, you weren't kidding about living simply, were you?" Choo-Choo leaned against the door frame of her shack. "What do you call this? Florida Minimal?"

"More like 'rent-free shit-hole that comes with the job.'"

Choo-Choo made a noncommittal sound and walked the floor. Ten strides took him to the far wall, where a hotplate sat atop a tiny square fridge beside a rusted sink. He looked over the plastic bins that protected the little food on hand. His fingers ghosted over the mosquito netting that draped the crooked aluminum cot.

"Rats?"

"Sometimes."

"Cockroaches?"

"Palmetto bugs. The size of dinner plates."

"TV?"

"No."

"Wi-Fi?"

"At the bar."

"Can you get phone reception?"

"I don't know. I don't have a phone." She shrugged when he looked up at her. "Who would I call?" He said nothing, just kept trailing his fingers over surfaces. "Do you hate it?"

The mosquito netting bunched up beneath his fingers as he moved over the contours of a large conch shell sitting in a sand-filled tray on the nightstand. He followed the narrowing curve of the shell and dug his fingers into the sand.

Dani had fitted a broken mop handle into the sharp-edged shell and filled it with quick-drying concrete. Choo-Choo hefted the homemade mace.

He smiled. "It's starting to grow on me." He buried the handle, smoothing his fingers over the sand to cover his tracks. "Do they come to check on you? The Feds? Me too, for a while. They came under the guise of following up on my story. They didn't stay long. The truth is the FBI is a bit below the pay grade of the security that usually accompanies my family. I'm not sure which my father was more embarrassed about—me being a junkie or me being of interest to something as pedestrian as the Bureau. I'm under the impression that phone calls were made and assurances given that I would behave."

"What will they do when they find out you've run away to Florida with a stranger?"

"Assume it's situation normal. Assume that I'm fucking up again." He leaned against the open window and considered her. "But what about you? What is all this glamour? What's the story with you and Papaw at the bar?"

"Mr. Randolph. He's my boss. He's good to me." She shook her head at Choo-Choo's smirk. "Not like that. He pays me okay and the work is good. Bartending and housekeeping."

"Like your mom."

She smiled. "You remembered. Yeah, like my mom."

"And how about your dad? Still doing any of the little tricks he taught you?"

Dani laughed and looked out the window. "You really don't forget much, do you?"

"Nothing juicy like your mad cold-reader skills. I figure you're working in a bar again, lots of tourists. Could be pretty lucrative. And nicely outside the letter of the law."

"Nothing like that. Well, not too much. I don't want to put Mr. Randolph in an awkward position by victimizing his customers. But I've helped out here and there. Mr. Randolph has these meetings with people and I keep an eye on them."

"An eye?"

"Maybe a fingertip or two." Dani felt her face warm at the confession. "I forgot how easy it can be to empty pockets."

Choo-Choo laughed out loud. "Pickpocketing? I had no idea your skills ran so broad."

"I don't keep anything. I just read a little bit here and there, stuff they have in their briefcases and shirt pockets. And on their phones. And sometimes in their cars. I make sure it all finds its way back to them." She laughed again when she saw his grin. "Just trying to stay sharp, you know? It's not like I can use those skills in a legitimate job anymore."

The name Rasmund sat thick and ugly between them.

Dani shook her head. "I guess I never did, huh? Oh well, at least now I'm not working for anyone who fakes it. I'm working a meeting this morning with two bad dudes who've got everyone on edge here. A couple of psychos from Miami."

"Psycho how?"

"Crazy. Gun-happy. Tweaked beyond belief but, I don't know, they don't scare me that much. I mean, I don't want to cross them, but they're just garden-variety tweakers with guns. They're straight-forward animals. Not what you'd call cunning."

Choo-Choo slid his fingers along the bottom of the windowsill and Dani watched as he detached a thin strip of stainless steel she had hidden there. He didn't flinch when he cut himself on one of the edges she had honed to a razor's edge.

He looked at himself in the reflection of the metal. "Well, if anyone would know cunning, it would be you."

CHAPTER EIGHT

Oren swore into his glass when Caldwell strolled into the bar. He'd forgotten to tell his buddy that the Wheeler meeting hadn't gone down yesterday. Caldwell wanted an update and knew better than to do it on the phone. Now Oren had an FBI agent in his bar and the Wheelers on the way. If that Bermingham cat tried to pull something, Oren didn't want to guarantee anyone's safety around Juan and Joaquin.

"What's the good news?" Caldwell climbed onto his stool, throwing out his customary greeting without looking.

"Don't have a lick of it." Oren's expected response. Then, voice lowered: "Our Canadian friend is not happy about the meeting being put off a day. And Juan is not happy with the way Bermingham spoke to him on the phone when Juan gave him the news, which, of course, gets Joaquin excited, thinking that heads are going to roll. And an excited Joaquin Wheeler is an unsavory sight."

"From what I've been able to unearth, that's SOP for Vincente. Makes people wait. Gets them on edge. Makes them screw up."

"It's a good plan unless the screwup involves a couple of dusted-up sadists with guns."

Caldwell nodded. "It seems Bermingham's no stranger to that, even in his brief tenure as bad guy. They call him Baby Bermie and he's a rising star. Took down a couple of big operations through Detroit and Windsor, all the way to Buffalo. Word is he wants to move Vincente out and take over Miami. He hits hard and fast, and the people that do survive working with him are suddenly struck with a lifelong inability to remember his face."

"That's a nice skill." Oren closed his eyes. "What do you figure he uses? Hypnosis?"

Caldwell chuckled. "Probably something more along the lines of aversion therapy. Which is why I completely understand if you are unable to get a picture of his face for me."

Oren just sighed. He was a big believer in the power of aversion therapy. "What do you suppose he's doing all the way down here? That's a big territory gap. Don't they have enough heroin in Canada?"

"The bad news is I haven't told you the bad news yet. I can't get any of my usual sources to tell me anything definite about what Vincente's moving, but he has something Bermingham wants and he wants it badly. It's a safe bet it isn't antiques and I'm getting a bad feeling it isn't drugs either. And Vincente is using this heat wave to put the screws to the deal."

"The heat? What's that got to do with anything? Surely Bermingham can afford air conditioning and a bag of ice."

"Whatever they're moving doesn't do well in the heat."

Oren rolled his glass between his palms. "No chance we're talking about an illegal shipment of gourmet cheese, huh?"

"Not likely. And not likely to be coming up from points south. Good cheese is usually from the north." Caldwell took a sip from Oren's glass and grimaced. "No, my friend, I think the reason the Wheelers have such a hard-on for this gig is that they're rising in Vincente's ranks. Simon Vincente has his fingers in a lot of nasty pies and I have a bad feeling this particular deal involves a shipment of things that go boom."

"Nice to know I can still be surprised." Oren upended his glass. "Wait. Explosives? Who would Canada be bombing?"

Caldwell laughed. "Terrorists these days like to shop around. Maybe the Canadian dollar gives them a better rate on the international market. I don't get the impression either Bermingham or Vincente are what you'd call patriots to their respective flags."

"Well Juan and Bermingham are putting the finals on the deal at ten thirty this morning," Oren said. Peg was nowhere in sight, and Dani was still showing Mr. Tiger Beat around. Nobody seemed in a hurry to get their next drink. "At least we won't have long to worry."

X X X

<u>7:40am, 89° F</u>

Dani drew back the mosquito netting, tying it into a thick knot to give them both a little more room in the cramped shack. Less than ten feet long and twelve feet wide, every inch of the refurbished space came in handy. Choo-Choo leaned sideways on the cot to reach the blue-and-gray yarn monstrosity hanging in place of what would have been the headboard.

"I'll bite," he said, his fingers dipping through loose stitches and over glittery appliquéd flowers. "Is this some sort of native dress?"

She laughed, looking away. She couldn't say why it made her uncomfortable to see someone touching the shawl. It was one of the few things she'd taken with her when she'd left DC. "Sort of, I guess. You might say it's a traditional trailer park ceremonial garb. When a Kenny Chesney T-shirt just won't do."

She should have known that Choo-Choo, with his scary-good hearing, would catch the tension in her voice. He'd been an audio analyst at Rasmund. They both had their talents. He wrapped a frayed tassel of gray fringe around his middle finger and looked back at her, cocking an elegant eyebrow.

"Remember how I told you that when I was little, my mom got sick?"

He nodded. "Mentally."

"Yeah, crazy." For some reason that made her relax. Choo-Choo had a way of making ugly things casual and hard things easy. "So while my dad was on the road, I went from relative to relative. We moved from Norman down to Flat Road and points south. I moved from house to house and trailer to trailer. Nobody treated me badly but everyone made it really clear that I was part of their Christian obligation."

"That sounds warm."

"Yeah. The one exception was my Aunt Penny. She was my mom's cousin's ex-wife or something. I'm really not sure, but they must have been pretty desperate to put her on the list of people who had to take me."

"Those Christian obligations do add up quickly, don't they?"

Dani nodded. "Aunt Penny drank and smoked and I'm not entirely sure she wasn't a prostitute on the side. She had a lot of men coming through there but was also really, really funny. She'd laugh all the time and I remember that she was the only person in all those years who was genuinely happy to see me show up on her doorstep. The rest of them thought I couldn't tell, but kids know, you know? They can feel it when someone is happy to see them and when someone isn't."

Choo-Choo stared at the ugly shawl as if he could see its history played out in the stitches. "And Aunt Penny made this for you?"

"No, nothing that heartwarming. She gave it to me." Dani straightened out a blue felt flower hanging by a thread. "Uncle Bill and Aunt Ruth were taking me to Aunt Penny, and I realized I'd left my coat at their house. It was my favorite. It was from Toronto and it had a cowboy stitched on the pocket. I cried and cried but Aunt Ruth said we were already an hour from their place and it was too far to go back and get it. I was still crying when we got to Aunt Penny's. She told me that she had something better than some old coat and pulled this out."

"And you thought it was gorgeous."

"No, I knew it was hideous." Choo-Choo snorted at that and Dani grinned. "I was eleven; I wasn't blind. But by then I knew to take my kindness where I could get it." She smoothed the lumpy knit against the wall and stepped away. "So now I take that ugly thing everywhere I go. I can't seem to get rid of it. I swear they're going to bury me in it. And speaking of taking things everywhere you go," Dani nodded at his backpack between his feet. "Did you bring clothes?"

Choo-Choo looked around the small shack. "Did you? Aside from your glamour-shawl?"

"They're in the bait shop. I usually just dress in there."

"I'll assume you have your reasons." He toed the canvas bag. "And yeah, I usually keep a couple things with me. It's not quite a Rasmund pouch but . . ."

"Comes in handy all the same, doesn't it?"

"You mean when someone swoops in to pluck you from your life?"

With Choo-Choo on the small cot, there wasn't anywhere else to sit except to hop up onto the little cabinet that served as her kitchen. "I guess I didn't think this through, bringing you down here. You can sleep on the cot. I don't really sleep that much."

"I was just going to say the same thing."

"About not thinking this through?"

"About not sleeping much." He smoothed the cheap sheets along the aluminum frame. "Beds are just sort of a prop for me these days."

"I sleep on the kayak dock." She tipped her head out toward the inlet. "Well, I lie on it and close my eyes for a while at least."

He lay back, unfolding himself and stretching long, the old cot barely creaking under his graceful motion. He stared up into the low ceiling beams. "It's weird, isn't it? This? Me being here. When you think about it, we hardly even know each other and yet you are the only person I've wanted to see for months. I have a confession to make."

Dani didn't trust herself to speak. She crossed her legs, folding herself up small, and waited for him to keep talking. He didn't seem to be in a hurry and when he did speak, she could barely hear him over the calls of the birds and rustle of the hot breeze through the date palms.

"When I couldn't find you, when I couldn't find anyone with your name in Oklahoma"—he closed his eyes and Dani had to lean forward to hear him—"I thought . . . I started to think that maybe you were in on it too."

She nearly fell forward, her disbelief coming out in a short, hard breath.

He draped his arm over his eyes. "I didn't know what to think. I knew I had to be careful. I couldn't go on a full-blown search for you. Feds were watching; my family was watching. I was busy kicking that whole brain-melting drug slavery thing they'd gifted me with. Maybe that's what made me paranoid, but I kept thinking about Rasmund and how we'd worked in that building where they were torturing political prisoners. Torturing them right under our feet. Right under our noses and we never knew. I never knew."

"I didn't know."

"I know. I know that now. I knew it then." He raised himself up on his elbows and looked at her. "I did. It's just that I was in there for so long and you were gone. They kept asking me these questions about you. I don't know if they were trying to plant seeds in my mind, playing some sort of fucked-up game to keep us from connecting again, or if I was just pissed off and needing someone to be mad at. Someone who didn't hold my life in their hand. And then I couldn't find you in Oklahoma. You said you were going back to

Oklahoma, and I couldn't find any trace of you there. I thought either you'd lied to me or that they'd done something to keep you from getting to Oklahoma." He dropped back down on the cot, shaking his head. "And I can't even tell you which one of those two was a worse thought to dwell on."

"I couldn't find you either."

He nodded. "But I didn't see you get shot."

He let the words hang there. Dani watched him lie still, his breathing even, his beautiful face smooth. Of all the things she'd expected to feel with Choo-Choo, anger wasn't one of them.

"What does that mean?"

"It means the last thing I saw was our boss ordering someone to pull the trigger. And I keep going back to those long phone conversations you kept having with Tom, the man our boss hired to kill us all. We were running for our lives and I heard you tell Tom that you trusted him. He was hired to kill us and you chatted with him over and over again that night."

"I didn't 'chat' with him, Choo-Choo." She gripped the edge of the counter, lowering her feet toward the ground. Ready to pounce on him. Punch him, pound on him, erase his suspicion with blood and broken bones. "You have no idea what happened that night."

"Tell me."

So she did. She told him everything.

She told him how Tom Booker, with his crisp white shirt and beautiful blue eyes, had shot their boss in front of her, then bantered with Dani like that cold, bloody night was a date. She told him how she'd run, her leg wounded from a ricochet, until he caught up with her at the Tidal Basin, pinned her against the wall. She spared no detail about the heat coming off of his body and the look in his eyes and the weird, hideous sense of seduction he'd given his threats.

She told him about the knife he thrust at her, stopped only by the Kevlar pouch she'd refused to leave behind, and how he'd then wrapped that pouch's strap around his neck to give her a chance to kill him before he killed her. She told him how soft his lips had felt underneath her thumb when she'd touched him, how he thought she had surrendered. And then she told him about throwing herself over the railing into the Tidal Basin to break Tom Booker's neck.

Then she stopped talking.

Choo-Choo sat up straight, his eyes wide. "You killed him?"

She dropped her gaze. "I thought I did. I wanted to. Maybe I did, but they told me I didn't. They told me he lived."

"They lie. Do you think he's dead?"

When she looked back up he was staring at her, leaning forward toward her. "It doesn't feel like it when I try to sleep. Or when I walk into the bar and there's a crowd and anyone has dark hair. Or when I hear footsteps behind me at night. Or when a cell phone rings."

He smiled. "So sleeping arrangements won't be a problem then."

XXX

8:10am, 89° F

"You cannot expect me to call a grown man Choo-Choo."

"Why not?" Dani looked him in the eye. "You call a grown man Rolly."

"That is not even in the same crazy-name ballpark, and you know it." Rolly, watching through the kitchen window, appeared to take some satisfaction in this. But then Rolly held up an egg sandwich for the pretty boy, and Oren surrendered. Why did he always feel like he had the least authority of anyone at this bar? "Sure, why not? Let's feed him. Let's give him a home and a job and maybe I can write him into my will."

He wanted to sound angrier, but the smile on Dani's face made that impossible. That was her real smile, not like that whatever-it-was with Caldwell. Of all the employees he'd ever had, she had done the most work with the least trouble. She wouldn't even let him improve the shack she slept in. If Dani wanted to find a way to cohabitate with some slick-as-snot pretty boy, so be it.

"But I'm not calling him or anyone Choo-Choo."

"That's okay, boss." Dani grabbed the plate. "He probably wouldn't answer anyway."

He watched her slide the plate before her friend, the two of them leaning over the food close enough to nearly touch foreheads. "You've still got to work my meeting this morning," Oren reminded her. "Ten thirty. I may need you to do, you know, what you do." She looked up long enough to nod. "Because this is all getting weird, you know? Something isn't right. This Bermingham is—" Rolly turned up the radio in the kitchen, and Oren sat back and looked around the bar. "Is anyone listening to me?"

CHAPTER NINE

8:14am, 89° F

Dani set Choo-Choo up with a gin and tonic. She knew Mr. Randolph wouldn't mind the tab, and Choo-Choo reasoned that the quinine would keep him from getting malaria. The idea of morning cocktails didn't seem to strike him as unusual at all. He looked relaxed at the bar, that weird hardness she'd seen on his face on Martha's Vineyard slipping just a shade. Maybe it was because she was relaxing for the first time in months. Here at Jinky's, now with Choo-Choo safe in her sights, it felt like she might just be able to plan on something other than running and hiding for the rest of her life.

When she saw the tall silhouette in the doorway off the deck, she felt that optimism grow. Tucker didn't look directly at her as their paths met at the far corner of the bar, but she could see those dimples trying to open up where he worked to keep his face neutral. She slid a napkin in front of him.

He settled on the barstool with an awkward arrangement of long legs and arms and elbows and knees that made Dani laugh. He pointedly didn't look at her, instead perusing the liquor shelf, but his dimples finally broke free. She had to resist the urge to push a soft lock of brown hair back from his forehead as he leaned in and whispered.

"So what do they drink on Martha's Vineyard?"

"I don't know. I didn't stick around to find out."

"Oh, just took your excuse to dodge me and ran with it?"

Dani leaned forward on her elbows. "Really? You think that's what I did?"

"I don't know." He finally looked her in the eye, his smile teasing. "You were in a pretty big hurry to get away from me yesterday."

"I had to do something important, and last night was my only chance to do it."

"Something important, huh? Important enough to fly all the way to Massachusetts? Must have been really important. So I take it that there's more to Dani Britton than just good legs and cold beer. What?" He leaned back from the bar. "Did I say something wrong?"

She glued a smile in place. "How did you know my last name?"

"Uh, you told me?"

"No." She tried to keep her tone casual, the fact-checker in her brain running through their conversation yesterday. She forced her fingers not to grip the edge of the bar. She knew she hadn't told him her last name; her habit of keeping personal information to an absolute minimum was a hard-worn habit. "I didn't tell you."

Tucker covered his eyes with his hand, squinting as he rubbed his brow. Dani's neck tensed to the point of aching until he lowered his hand and stared seriously at her.

"There is a better-than-average chance that I might be stalking you." He held up his thumb and forefinger. "Just a little bit." When she didn't laugh with him, he looked embarrassed. "Okay, I asked your boss, the guy with the white hair. Is that your dad? Because he didn't exactly gush information about you. I asked him if you were seeing anyone and he said if I didn't have the stones to ask you myself,

I probably didn't have the stones to go out with you. I'm not really sure what that means. Are you married?"

"No."

"Divorced? Crazy ex?"

"No."

Tucker leaned in. "Are you gay?"

"What? No."

"Are you a man?" He leaned in closer. "Were you a man?"

Dani laughed. "No. I'm not a man."

"Whew." Tucker rested his chin in his palm, considering her. "Then why would it be so scary to go out with you? Hmm? Or were you doing something incredibly wicked in Boston?"

"It was Martha's Vineyard and it was no big deal. I just had to get a friend of mine." She tipped her head in Choo-Choo's direction. "A friend."

He squinted at her with mock seriousness. "Good, because I think you're really cute. And I'm not good at this, you know. I work all the time. I'm always traveling. All the women I meet are clients or coworkers and everyone's got business cards and resumes. And yours is the first thigh I've ever eaten mango salad off of." Dani felt her face warm. "And it would really, really suck if you were shady. Or a guy."

Dani shook her head. "Well, speaking of cute, you are very cute. And you're here very early. I thought you rode in on the *Lady of Spain* yesterday."

"Nah." He shook his head. "My buddy Ned and I were just checking out the Keys between client calls. We decided to crash here last night."

"Here? At the camp? Uh-oh. That means I didn't make up your room."

Tucker made a scary face. "No, that biker chick did. Well, she handed us a key and threw a stack of sheets at us. I figured we were lucky to get out alive."

Dani laughed. "Have a beer with me. Beer for breakfast. My treat." She grabbed two Coronas from the cooler, ignoring Tucker's flicker of disapproval at her choice. "Drink it. It won't kill you. You don't even have to have the lime if you don't want."

He sighed dramatically. "The things I do for you." They clinked bottles and drank deep. "So you flew all the way to Martha's Vineyard for what? That guy? Who's not your boyfriend?"

"He's a friend and he needed me so I went to get him."

Tucker leaned forward on his elbows once more, coming close to Dani's face. "So if you and I become friends, will you come flying in to save me?"

Now it was Dani's turn to be coy. She rolled the bottle on its edge. "I don't know. He and I are really good friends."

He gave a soft laugh. "We could be really good friends too, right? I mean, I'm only here until Friday so we'll have to get kind of serious about, you know, getting to know each other."

"Until Friday, huh? Tomorrow? That's not very long. And don't you have to work?" When he shrugged, she nudged his hand with hers, letting her knuckles rest against his. "What is it you do, anyway, that sends you down here and calls it business?"

"My job? Look, when I say I want to sleep with you it doesn't mean I want to put you to sleep. Oh my God." He set his bottle down hard. "Was that rude? I totally didn't mean for that to come out like that. I am so sorry."

Dani's stomach tightened with a delicious twist as she giggled. This guy was absolutely adorable and she had never really cared for adorable guys before. He looked so embarrassed by his comment and she started to wonder how long it had been since she'd seen anyone show anything like modesty or decorum or even just social nicety. For years she'd worked with spies—she'd thought they were just corporate spies, but nonetheless—watching people who were probably committing corporate espionage. Before that had been skeevy bars in Oklahoma and before that summers in a truck with her dad. No scenes in her life had ever been populated by long-legged, floppy-haired, dimple-faced sweet guys who blushed at being too forward.

She could get used to this.

Tucker struggled to get the conversation back on track. "Yeah, so my job—I guess you could say a lot of it is data analysis."

"Oh!" She caught herself before blurting out that she used to have a similar job. That wasn't a conversation she wanted to start. She started to say something instead about how interesting that sounded when she saw movement at the other end of the bar.

She could only manage one word.

"Shit."

Agent Crawford had his arm around Choo-Choo.

X X X

_8:45am, 91° F_

"I've got to keep Dani out of this meeting." Oren pushed his empty glass between his fingers. "She's got a good head on her shoulders but I think these guys are just too unpredictable." Caldwell made a strange humming sound. "I know that sound. That's your bullshit-on-the-horizon warning."

"I'm not saying bullshit, Oren." The agent kept his voice as low as Oren's so they wouldn't be overheard by Dani's blond friend sitting several seats away. "I'm just saying I wouldn't be surprised to learn that there's something not one hundred percent aboveboard with your girl."

"What did you find? I know you ran a background check. What is it?"

"Nothing." Caldwell looked Oren in the face. "Nothing."

"And? The absence of evidence proves what?"

The agent sighed. "If I do a check on you with the Bureau, I'll find your arrest records. I know because I've checked. There's also all the other stuff—employment history, contact info, driver's license stuff. The usual, but your file gets a special little flag because of your checkered history. We have tons of files like that."

"And Dani?"

"Danielle Kathleen Britton, twenty-eight, of Flat Road, Oklahoma. No arrests, no convictions, no felonious associations."

"Sounds treacherous."

Caldwell seemed to measure his words. "Sounds perfectly harmless. I'm just thinking about a good girl like that finding this impossible-to-find place and working so hard for so little. I know how much you pay, you cheap bastard, yet here she is. Loyal and good. And well-established when a new bad guy decides to move in on Vincente."

"What are you talking about?"

"Bermingham, the new big gun coming down from the north. Nobody knows him. He seems to get into places nobody gets into and leaves untouched. Your girl shows up and so does Bermingham."

"Six months later."

"After you've exposed Dani to most of your usual business associates." He nodded at Oren. "I know about you using her to work your meetings. I've heard some stories. It seems like she has some other skills besides bartending. All I'm saying is be careful. Watch for things that don't add up. Like the deal being moved down here instead of going down in Miami."

"Vincente changed the plans, not the Canadian."

"And you know this how?" Caldwell asked. "Because you overheard Juan Wheeler say so? How informed do you think the Wheelers really are? And just out of curiosity, was Dani around during that phone call? When Juan passed you money?"

"No." Oren shook his head. "I mean, she brought us drinks. It's her job."

"Uh-huh. Okay. Then you have nothing to worry about. But watch for signs. Don't let your guard down because she's little and cute. Little and cute can still pull a great big trigger, or get one pulled, and I can't always protect you."

Oren wanted to throw Caldwell out. He wanted to yell at him that he was a suspicious old prick who didn't know his ass from a hole in the ground. He wanted to say that Dani was becoming like a daughter to him.

Instead he said, "What signs?"

"A willingness to stick around a situation any sane person would avoid."

"Like a meeting with the Wheelers."

Caldwell nodded. "I was thinking more about living in that shitty shack, but yeah."

"What else?"

"New people hanging around because of her."

"This is a tourist bar on a tourist island in the biggest tourism state in the country."

Caldwell's gaze rested on the sullen blond nursing his drink in the middle of the bar. "People who are here because of her. People you don't know but that she vouches for."

Oren put his head in his hands. "Shit."

"Let me see what I can do, Oren. Let's see what this kid's made of." Caldwell downed his drink and grinned. "A little friendly bar chat. This is a friendly bar, after all. Let's be friendly."

Oren watched. When Caldwell rose and headed his way, the expression on the kid's face didn't exactly change; it sort of solidified. Whoever Dani's friend was, he knew how to keep his guard up.

"Hey pal, how you doing?" Caldwell asked.

"Terrific. *Pal.*" The words slid out cold as glaciers from the kid's lips. "How are you?"

The agent stood aggressively close.

"Oren tells me your name is Choo-Choo. What kind of name is Choo-Choo?"

"A fun one."

The agent's smile widened and sharpened. "It is a fun one. This is a fun place." A rough slap to the back, rougher than could be called chummy, and the kid didn't flinch. "What are you drinking?"

The kid sighed, obviously having enough sense to know that wherever this conversation was headed, it was inevitable. "Tanqueray and tonic. Lots of lime. Want one?"

"That looks good." Caldwell took the drink from the kid's fingers, smelling it and putting it back on the bar. "Did Dani make it for you? She makes a good drink, doesn't she?" He leaned on his elbows, smiling at the kid. "I bet she knows just how you like your drink, doesn't she?"

"Indeed." The blond's smile wasn't much of an improvement in the warmth department. "Rumor has it that you can order your drink any way you like it, and she'll make it that way. It's just like Christmas every day of the week."

Oren watched the body language of the two men, Caldwell forcibly cheerful, the blond politely sullen. The agent narrowed his eyes and Oren flashed back to a dozen unpleasant encounters of his own with the law. He was glad he didn't have to endure these kinds of head games anymore. Before Caldwell could decide just how far he wanted to take this, Casper van Dosen strolled in off the deck, waving his hands in time to his off-tune humming of "Lady of Spain."

"Don't get up! Don't rise for me!" he shouted toward the bar, holding up his hands, although nobody had made a move to rise for him. "This is not a business visit. I am here strictly for social reasons."

Oren smiled at the wind-burned little man, taking in his bandy legs sticking out from frayed cotton shorts, his loud Hawaiian shirt showing tufts of white chest hair against his too tan skin. Casper launched himself onto his regular stool.

"What's the matter, Casper?" Oren asked, glad for a distraction from wherever Caldwell was headed. "Nobody taking you up on your sunrise cruises today?"

"Taking me up? Are you mad?" Casper slammed his palm on the bar. "I've got them lined up three deep on the edge of Big Pine but I was forced to sneak off without them this morning. Forced to sneak off like a thief in the night. Or the dawn, as the case may be." He glanced down the bar where Dani stood talking with the tall fellow from yesterday. "Dani, my dear, is that a gin and tonic I spy in our young friend's hand?"

"It is, Casper," Dani said with a smile. "Do you think I might be able to talk you into one? Tonic water is a powerful curative on a day like this."

"Dani, my dear, I believe you could talk me into just about anything. And I appreciate your concerns for my health." He pointed to the blond kid. "And how about another one for our young friend here. Will you have a drink with me?"

Oren watched the kid turn his back on Caldwell, draping himself on an elbow. From what Oren could see of his face, that was probably the closest thing to a real smile the kid could muster. "I believe I will."

"Well now that's just fantastic. Fantastic." He watched Dani pour the drinks. When she slid the second down the bar to the blond, he held up his glass for a toast. "And what is it they call you, my friend?"

Before the kid could speak, Caldwell clamped a hand on his shoulder and shouted him down. "They call him Choo-Choo. Choo-Choo! You ever heard such a name? He's a friend of Dani's, just showed up today, and wants us all to call him Choo-Choo."

The captain seemed to consider the question. Oren knew the rummy act wasn't entirely a front, but the old captain was a lot brighter than he let on. And Oren knew what Caldwell didn't—if there was one thing Casper van Dosen couldn't stand, it was a bully. Caldwell had just given Dani's friend another ally.

"Any friend of Dani's is a friend of mine and I think Choo-Choo is an outstanding name!" The old man raised his drink and the kid followed suit. "It speaks of the magnificent tradition of the rails that made this country great. It speaks of travel and voyages—and speaking of voyages," he leaned toward the kid and lowered his voice. "Do you have any love of the water?"

The kid leaned toward him in turn. "I could sail before I could drive."

"Well then, this is an auspicious encounter. I've been forced to postpone my sunrise cruise because my first mate is having a tiff with his very unpleasant and very pregnant girlfriend, leaving me without a crew for the day, if not for the foreseeable future. I can't legally conduct my business without a first mate, and I would sorely hate to miss the sunset on a hot day like this. Could I interest you in a position on the world-famous *Lady of Spain* Party Pontoon?"

The kid raised his glass. "Auspicious indeed. Just tell me where and when."

"I'll admit I had come by here today to lure the always dependable Dani into service but it seems destiny has intervened," he said to the blond. "I can't guarantee full-time employment and the only benefits you get are the open water and all the sweet flesh the complimentary margaritas open up for you, but a man could do a lot worse in terms of gainful employment."

The boy smiled at Dani and then nodded. "I've had worse jobs. Trust me."

Casper toasted and drained his drink. "You're a good man, Choo-Choo, and that's a fine name. Come on over to Big Pine and follow the signs for the *Lady of Spain* this afternoon." He got to his feet and patted Choo-Choo on the cheek. "Oh the ladies are gonna love you, boy. Almost as much as they love the margaritas and the captain. First Mate Choo-Choo, welcome aboard the *Lady of Spain*."

"Aye, aye, Captain."

Casper laughed, clapping the kid on the shoulder with a much kinder touch than Caldwell's. The little captain eyed the agent with a look of triumph and a little bit of warning. Casper might seem to be just a mouthy little drunk, but he was a local legend; he loved his Keys and he loved his bars and he loved the people who filled both. Caldwell's tough-guy tactics hadn't won him any friends today.

The kid smirked into his drink as Casper strolled out of the bar whistling the same tune he'd entered on. Caldwell stared into the bar mirror, watching Casper disappear and the kid finish his drink.

"Well that worked out pretty well for you, didn't it, Choo-Choo?" He drew out the name, separating the words to sarcastic effect. "Just hours here and you've got a job. A title, even."

Oren watched the kid smile into his glass before turning that smile up at Caldwell. Oren had seen colder smiles in his life but not many.

"I do have a title now and everyone in this bar knows it." He leaned in toward Caldwell as if going for a kiss. Instead he whispered loud enough for Oren to overhear. "I wonder if you can say the same, *agent.*"

Caldwell made a sound of disbelief, shaking his head as if he'd never heard anything so ridiculous, but if Oren could see the flush of heat rising on the agent's face, the kid certainly could. Caldwell picked up his drink and headed back toward his stool. As he stepped behind him, Oren could hear one word escape on a breath.

"Shit."

CHAPTER TEN

9:00am, 93° F

Choo-Choo shook his head at Dani as Caldwell took his seat beside Mr. Randolph. She should have told him about Caldwell, but from the look of disgust on his face, it seemed he hadn't had any trouble figuring it out. It hadn't taken the agent long to swoop in. If Caldwell knew who Choo-Choo was, he had to know more about Dani than she'd originally suspected. Could he do something about it? Was he going to scamper back to his little hidey-hole and report to the powers-that-be about the insidious collusion occurring at Jinky's? The thought punched a hole in her mood, every bit of her earlier optimism draining to the floor.

This was never going to change. She and Choo-Choo were never going to be out from under their thumb.

"Shit."

"My thoughts exactly." Tucker looked up from his phone. "Although I think we're talking about two different things."

"I'm sorry. There's just this thing." Dani waved it off.

"Another thing? You've got a lot of things going on, don't you?"

"Yeah, I do." Dani wasn't in the mood for any more playful banter. Maybe Mr. Randolph was right. If he needed constant

102

reassurance, maybe Tucker didn't have the stones to date her. She wiped at the bar with rough strokes.

He downed the rest of his beer and stood, shifting from one foot to the other. "Look, I've got to go meet some people and actually make a living for a little while. I don't know how long it's going to take. Can I get your number?"

"I don't have a phone."

His eyes widened. "Really? Is that even allowed anymore?"

She shrugged, not looking up. "Everyone I know is right here."

"Yeah, but now you know me, and I'm leaving, so . . ."

She looked past him to see Caldwell head out and off the deck, taking a chunk of her tension with him. Tucker stood waiting, looking unsure. None of this was his fault. Maybe she shouldn't require everyone to have such big stones.

"So . . ." She leaned forward against the bar. "Come back. I'm always here."

He started to speak, but a beep from his phone cut him off. He glared at it. "I've got to take this. Can you —I mean, just . . . hang on." He put the phone to his ear and headed out to the deck. Dani wiped up the bar, tossing their bottles, postponing a look down the bar.

Choo-Choo sat with his chin in his palms, his fingertips pressed against his eyelids. His high spirits over his job offer long gone. If ever there was a posture that screamed, "Leave me alone," that was it. Mr. Randolph pushed away from the bar and it seemed to her he made a point of not meeting her eye. That could mean Caldwell had told him something about her. Something that may or may not be true. Caldwell had certainly said something to Choo-Choo and, true or not, it hadn't been friendly.

Everything was going to fall apart.

That familiar tumbling fear rushed over her. She had nothing to count on. Nothing ever stayed where it was. She had no place to hide and had no control over the forces against her.

This wasn't a new fear. This wasn't even just the result of the betrayal at Rasmund. This was a lesson she had been learning her entire life. From the time her mother's mental illness took hold, forcing her to be shuttled from relative to relative waiting for her father to come off the road to take her away, Dani had learned to contain this fear, to put it in a little compartment in her mind so that the rest of her thoughts could function and behave and move her through her life. She could feel her mind shoving and stomping on the fear beast, wrestling it into its cage, but for some reason, today she wouldn't let it be tamed.

Not for some reason.

She knew why.

She didn't want to contain the beast. She didn't care what she'd been forced to accept as a fact all her life. Dani didn't want it to be true anymore.

She wanted to stay.

Dani winced as the bar rag she'd been twisting in her grip finally cut off the circulation to her fingers. Daring to admit those words to herself made her want to hide under the bar. She wanted to scream and throw glass after glass just to hear them shatter. A shadow passed across the floor of the bar and Dani looked up.

She wanted something else too.

Without giving herself a chance to talk herself out of it, Dani jumped up onto the bar, swung her legs over, and threw herself down on the other side. She didn't stop to right the stool she kicked over on the way and thought she might have heard Mr. Randolph yell to her, but she ran from the bar.

There on the steps leading down from the deck stood Tucker, still on the phone. He didn't see her until she stood on the top of the steps and when he noticed her, he smiled, those big dimples winking at her. He held up a finger, asking her to wait, and Dani really hoped he wouldn't be long. She didn't want to lose her nerve.

"Yeah, yeah, yeah, okay." Tucker made an impatient gesture, smiling at Dani as if he could read her mind. "Yeah, I got it. I'm there. We're good. I gotta go. Okay. Okay, yeah. Sheesh." He ended the call with a flourish. "Yakity-yak. Someone needs to learn to text."

Now that he was off the phone and she had his full attention, Dani didn't know what to do. Even standing two steps above him, she was barely level with his face. His smile changed from happy surprise to something a little more knowing as he leaned up the steps toward her.

"Hi."

Oh she was so bad at this. "If I had a phone, I would give you my number."

He laughed. "I'd like to have it, Dani. I'd like to know more about you, what you do here." He stepped closer, bending to keep his face close to hers. "I'd like to know a lot more about you. What you're good at. What you like."

She couldn't really make any sense of his words, distracted as she was by the nearness of his face and the gold and green flecks she could see in his brown eyes, so she just let her gaze move to his dimples and let him get closer as he spoke.

"So far I know you drink shitty beer and good gin. I know you look really cute in your little dresses and shorts and that you're allowed to sit on the bar." His nose brushed against hers and she could smell the beer on his breath as he whispered, "What else do you do around here?"

She closed her eyes, letting her cheek brush against his. "Um, catch rats?"

"What?" He pulled back a little, squinting to focus on her.

Dani felt her face redden. God, how bad had she gotten at flirting? She used to be good at it. "In the units. That's part of my job." She waved her hand in the general direction of the rental units. "And I clean. I'm the housekeeper. Not very cool."

Tucker tilted his head, considering her. "I think you're pretty cool. And I think you probably do a lot of things that are cooler than cleaning house and catching rats."

Before she could protest, he kissed her. It was a soft kiss that lasted just long enough to make her sigh. Before she could think enough to wonder how she should react, he kissed her again, this one not so soft. He followed it with a third kiss that drove every thought out of her head except riding the kiss out to the end. When he pulled away, they were both grinning.

"I'll see you later?" he asked.

She nodded and watched him back down the steps. He flashed those dimples at her before he disappeared toward the parking lot. Dani stood there a moment, staring at the place he'd been standing, letting the sea breeze blow her hair off of her face. Her thoughts made no move to lock themselves into compartments.

XXX

Hartsfield-Jackson Atlanta International Airport
9:00am, 73° F

Booker retrieved his yarn bag from the security belt, thankful the guard hadn't seen the need to check its contents. There was nothing in the bag of interest to airport security, nothing but yarn, a crochet hook, and a tiny pair of yarn clippers. And the yellow afghan, of course. Booker would have kept his cool had the agents decided they needed to fondle his gift for Dani but it wouldn't have been easy. He could feel the tension sitting hard and hot at the base of his neck.

His employers didn't know where he was. They thought he was lying low because of his vague reference to heat after the hit on Agent Davis. That idiot had made the job absurdly easy, buying without question his convoluted lie about explosives and trackers and amphetamine shots. He couldn't resent the stupid man, although it had taken the entire drive with the windows down to get the smell of that filthy food out of Dani's afghan. Davis had come across for him with an address. Redemption Key, Florida.

Booker knew he could have searched for Dani himself. He still had resources. As the agent had said, any private investigator could have found her. She didn't seem to be hiding, working aboveboard and all. He squeezed the handle of the yarn bag more tightly at that thought. She still wasn't scared of them. Dani Britton, still showing up for work, still paying her taxes. He could imagine what she'd have to say about that, her hard-earned money going to pay Uncle Sam. He wished he could hear her say it.

Booker checked the screen at the gate. They'd be boarding in a little while, but he had time to pick up a few things for Florida. Florida, what was she doing in Florida?

He could have tracked her before this. Any private investigator could have found her; he could have found her with enough time. But while Booker knew the FBI had their fair share of morons like Agent Gregory Davis, he didn't imagine for one minute that the power behind the power employed many. They might not have seemed interested in his relationship with Dani—and really, it was a relationship, wasn't it?—but Booker wouldn't risk setting off any alarms.

Except for a few money transactions and retrieving a dormant ID he'd kept set aside for emergencies, Booker hadn't contacted any of his usual business associates. Fences, forgers, arms dealers—he wouldn't risk opening any of them up to federal investigation. No, Booker knew that if he bided his time and watched for an opportunity, someone would find Dani for him. And that Agent Davis had been planning on blackmailing his superior? That made him the perfect someone. Booker would bet his favorite little knife that the agent's laptop would arrive in the evidence locker mysteriously wiped of all memory and files.

Booker wheeled his nearly empty suitcase behind him toward

the clothing store. He'd ditched the laptop he'd had in Nashville so the bag weighed almost nothing with just his dress clothes in it. He'd had to ship his knives back home to a post office box. The damned airlines made carrying weapons so much more complicated. Still, he was headed to Florida, to a fishing camp, whatever that meant. Surely they sold knives for fishermen.

He could have driven. It wasn't like he was in any hurry. But once he'd had an address, an unfamiliar sense of urgency had flooded his body. He'd searched for flights to the Keys, found one from Nashville that got in at five o'clock in the afternoon. Then he'd found a non-stop from Atlanta that got in before noon.

He'd driven the three or so hours from Nashville to Atlanta in the middle of the night, telling himself it was an effective plan to shake his employers should they decide to track him. He assured himself that the identity he used to buy the ticket wouldn't set off any alarms. He told himself that by getting to Florida as quickly as possible, he lessened the chance of being missed.

What he didn't tell himself, what he couldn't tell himself, was that he needed to hurry and find Dani Britton, see her with his own eyes, before he lost his nerve.

X X X

Jinky's, FL
10:10am, 96° F

She managed to get her grin mostly under control by the time the meeting started an hour later. Juan Wheeler had staked out the deck not long after Tucker had left, and Joaquin had joined him at some point when Dani had been packing ice into a cooler for the Australians. Mr. Randolph had finally looked at her when he got the message that the meeting was on.

"It's about time." He poured himself a vodka, resting back against the cash register so Dani and Peg could move around him. "If Vincente had pushed this meeting back one more time, there would have been hell to pay. Bermingham would show up shooting or Joaquin would explode from the heat. Is the room ready?"

"Yep," Dani said, grabbing a bar bucket and filling it with ice. "I've put some bottles of Mexi-Coke in there for Juan. He wanted to get in and pick his seat. I didn't think you'd mind."

"No, no, that's good." Mr. Randolph nodded. "Keep him happy. Make him feel like a big shot because I know he's really raw about being disrespected by the Canadian. Ice the liquor, okay? This heat is making everyone edgy. This Bermingham is supposed to be bad news. I wish you didn't have to be part of this." Dani looked up when Mr. Randolph's words faded. He stared at her for a moment and then shook his head, heading out from behind the bar. "Well, you know what to do, don't you, Dani?"

It didn't sound like a question.

She did know what to do. She'd watch Mr. Randolph cross the short end of the inlet to the cinder block unit and go into the room. Once he closed the door, she'd go back to the bar, gather her bucket, and stay out of sight until she heard the door slam once more. That meant Bermingham and his people were inside. New clients always wanted to come in unseen.

She'd wait a little longer, let her boss take control of the room and get everyone settled, then she would come in with ice and some better liquor in the bucket and let Mr. Randolph play gracious host. She'd take her cues from him, watching the participants in the meeting, avoiding Joaquin Wheeler's thick hands, and if anyone on the Canadian's side let any sort of information hang out of their pockets or on their phones, she'd read what she could. Most importantly, she'd read her boss, watch for any signals from him.

The door slammed and she waited. She rolled the vodka, rum,

and tequila bottles in the ice so the labels could be read, killing time until she felt she'd waited enough. She knew Juan had taken the power seat in the room, sitting on the far side of the small table, facing the door. Mr. Randolph would be on his right, mostly out of sight as the door swung open, so that the newcomers, Bermingham and whoever he brought, would be the first visible when she came through. Dani's father had called that position "first swing" when he used to sneak her into poker games. It was the most vulnerable position in a room.

Dani headed down the steps and across the inlet. She took a deep breath to steady herself before she pushed the door open. She wasn't afraid, not really, but more than once the people in the first swing spot had drawn weapons on her, and it helped to be ready. Dani knew to keep her head down, not looking at anyone until she found Mr. Randolph. Then she'd raise her eyes, get a feel for the temperature in the room, and let him introduce her or not, as he saw fit.

She pushed the door open. She heard the sudden halt to the conversation and was pretty certain at least one gun was raised. Pushing the door closed, she swung the bucket and looked across the floor for Mr. Randolph's sandals. When she raised her eyes and saw the expression on his face, she felt a knot of fear punch at her stomach.

"I think everyone here knows Dani, am I right?"

She turned her head slowly. Joaquin grinned at her, his one good eye winking. Next to him, Juan perched on the edge of his chair, scowling. A sandy-haired man in a black T-shirt stood with his muscular arms folded and straining his sleeves. Before she could think how she knew him, her gaze moved to the man sprawled in the chair in front of him.

Dani felt the handle of the bucket grow damp in her palms as she stared into the smiling brown eyes. He didn't show any teeth but the dimples wouldn't be held back.

"Hey Dani," Tucker said. "Good to see you again."

Not Tucker. Bermingham.

CHAPTER ELEVEN

She didn't even blink. Oren watched and she didn't even blink. Dani hadn't ever shown what he would call a wealth of expressiveness, but being face-to-face with proof that she'd kept her knowledge about the Canadian gangster from him when he'd asked her point-blank if she knew the guy, Oren would have hoped for at least a fumble of shame. But he didn't get it. He got nothing but the usual stone-face.

Bermingham certainly knew the score. Sprawled out in his chair, the big son of a bitch dwarfed the little table. His thug sidekick kept his piece tucked somewhere in the recess of his meaty armpit, and Bermingham didn't even seem to be carrying. Oren figured he probably had something ugly stashed in the enormous pockets of his cargo shorts.

Cargo shorts. And a golf shirt.

Canadian gangsters.

If it weren't so disturbing, Oren would laugh.

He wanted to listen to what they said to each other, listen through the posturing and the chest-thumping coming from the Wheeler boys.

Oren knew them well enough to know that Juan's temper toed the breaking point and Joaquin could smell it. The bigger Wheeler's face glistened with the oily sheen of anticipation that Oren knew was often the last thing his victims ever saw. Joaquin wanted this deal to go bad—he always did, because he loved the violence that followed—but Juan was nervous. Whatever this deal was, Juan Wheeler wanted it badly.

Dani poured Bermingham a shot of tequila and he smiled at her. At least she had the decency to not smile back, and that seemed to amuse the Canadian. He toasted the Wheelers and Oren and threw the shot back with a grimace.

He sucked on a lemon and squeezed his eyes shut. "Wow I don't know how you guys do this every day." He smacked his lips, laughing like they were knocking shots back at a bachelor party. "Give me a rye and ginger ale, eh? Or at least a beer, am I right, Ned? Something brown and serious, you know?"

It seemed Juan didn't care for the frat-house act any more than Oren did. The little man kicked his chair back, sweeping the table clean of glasses with one scarred and tattooed arm, the other swinging a Glock up into Bermingham's face.

"I don't give a fuck what you drink, you overgrown piece of—"

He didn't get to finish his sentence. Bermingham let Juan get to the creative part of the insult and then lunged from his seat with a speed Oren wouldn't have expected from a man his size. He slapped the gun aside, grabbing that wrist, and yanking Juan stomach first across the table. He twisted the gun hand at an ugly angle and pressed the muzzle against Juan's side.

Joaquin and Ned, Bermingham's thug, stood with guns drawn on each other, and Oren and Dani backed away. Juan struggled in the arm lock, wheezing for breath with Bermingham's fist jammed into the small of his back.

"You feel that, Juan?" He torqued Juan's wrist, pressing the gun harder into his side. "I'm gonna shoot your brother through your liver. Which one of you do you think will die first?" He let Juan swear and struggle, his feet useless off the floor. Oren could see that Bermingham's golf shirt hid an impressive muscular form. Bermingham only looked like a frat boy.

"Why don't you relax, you stupid fuck?" Bermingham spoke close to Juan's ear. "I don't think Mr. Randolph wants to be cleaning blood up out of these nice carpets, do you? It's bad enough Dani has to clean up the liquor you just spilled. What kind of fuck wastes good booze? Sheesh."

Bermingham straightened up, pulling back from the spinal punch he'd kept on Juan, but keeping his arm in the lock. "Now we've got business to do, and Mr. Randolph here was kind enough to let us use his place, so let's get it done. You've got Vincente's product; I've got money; we all win." He included Oren in his glance. "We all win. Alright? Okay, here we go."

He let go of Juan's arm, giving him a chummy slap on the shoulder as the little man squirmed off the table. No sooner had his feet hit the ground than Juan again pointed his weapon at Bermingham. The Canadian rolled his eyes and waved it off, settling back into his seat as if nothing had happened. His thug Ned holstered his piece as well, and Oren had to admit the Wheelers looked a little foolish, keyed-up and armed in the face of the Canadian's nonchalance.

It took balls to ignore that much sweaty-handed gun-power.

Bermingham gave the Wheelers a chance to save face, turning to Dani and asking for a fresh drink. And damn it if Dani didn't take it all in stride. She didn't flinch; she didn't hesitate. She just poured and served and stepped around the table to pick up the thrown glasses.

Dani and Bermingham and that pretty boy at the bar with the stupid name—Oren was being pushed around by an Abercrombie & Fitch catalog.

Those ridiculous dimples appeared once more as Juan took his seat and pushed Joaquin into his. Bermingham leaned back in his chair, sipping the fresh tequila Dani had poured. "So, twenty-five units. Still good, right?"

"Prime," Juan said, struggling to restore his gangster face. "You seen the pictures."

"Yeah I did, but that was three days ago. How do I know you're taking care of my cargo? I mean, this fucking heat, you got it in any kind of climate control?"

"We got vents on it."

"Vents, yeah." Bermingham scratched his face and leaned across the table. "Because here's the thing. If I find out you dipshits are storing my product on a boat in this heat before the deal goes down, the money goes bye-bye. I'm buying twenty-five units prime. Not twenty-four, not twenty-three. It's a bundle deal. Twenty-five units in prime condition. Any of them go bad in this heat, they all go bad, you follow? I'll let Vincente take the heat for casualties."

"Yeah, yeah. We know our shit."

"Good." Bermingham smiled, looking back at Ned, who smiled too. "They know their shit. That's great, eh? Because here's how this works." His smile stayed in place but iced over as he looked at Juan. "I'm going to inspect each unit before I pay. For every one of them that's damaged, you lose a finger. For every one that's broken beyond repair, you lose a limb." He held his hand up, miming counting off on his fingers. "Twenty-five units. That's a lot of fingers."

Oren tried not to sigh when he saw Joaquin ticking off his fingers. He knew Bermingham saw it too.

"You think this is some kind of fucking joke, you grease bag?" Bermingham said this calmly, conversationally. Joaquin looked up from his counting to Bermingham's black stare, and blinked. "You and your brother think Vincente can protect you from me?" He was almost whispering now. "If this shipment goes bad, all three of you will be praying to die."

X X X

<u>*10:33am, 98° F*</u>

Dani had to look at her fingertips to be sure she had the glass in hand. It didn't surprise her. She couldn't feel her fingertips because her brain was busy. Her thoughts weren't just lining up into little boxes; they were throwing themselves into cages like frightened gorillas.

She had no idea what was going on.

Experience had taught her that until she did, she had to stay calm, stay small, and stay quiet. And to think.

Somehow this made sense. There was some way she was supposed to assemble the facts before her that would erase the confusion. Cute, clumsy Tucker, who had disarmed her enough to make her chase him onto the deck in hopes of a kiss, was really Bermingham, a bad guy so bad that the insane Wheeler boys feared him. He was making a deal so dangerous that Mr. Randolph was terrified. And Mr. Randolph was looking at her like she somehow played a part in all of this because Mr. Randolph's best friend was a federal agent who had obviously said something.

Lining the facts up wasn't helping.

She knew she was breathing because she could smell Juan's fear sweat when she scooped up the spilled ice near his feet. She never thought she'd long for the days when Juan's regular sour-feet-and-onion funk overpowered everything else. Bermingham kept talking, those broad northern vowels sounding so out of place in the heat.

"So yeah, I'll be spending a good bit of time around here until we're done. That's not going to be a problem, is it Oren?" Dani didn't bother to look up to see Mr. Randolph's nod. What else was he going to do? "Great. I want make myself available while the deal is going down just in case anyone gets nervous. I want to make it really clear that I've got everything covered. We're not having any more changes in plan. You tell Vincente."

"That's Mr. Vincente to you," Juan said.

"I'll call him my fucking prom date if I want to, okay? Great. Now you two boys catch a ride back to Miami, load my nice, cool cargo carefully into the *Pied Piper* and sail that baby gently to the inlet here. You bring her to shore no earlier than dawn, no later than nine in the morning. You don't take my boat or my cargo out in this fucking heat, or it will be the last mistake you ever make. If one goes bad, they all go bad, remember? I inspect the cargo and, if it's all sound, I transfer the money to Vincente's account before the banks close in Zürich. Everyone gets what they want before the weekend."

He turned to smile at Dani. "And we all want to have a good weekend, don't we?"

Chairs moved, people moved, Dani put bottles and empty glasses into the bucket. The Wheelers left first; without even looking, she could feel the heat of the glare Juan gave Mr. Randolph. When she did look, Mr. Randolph didn't look at her. She hauled the bucket toward the door, past Bermingham's long legs still stretched out in front of his chair, and stopped where her boss had no choice but to see her.

"Is it okay if I go for a run before my shift?"

"Sure." His voice sounded odd. "You can take the day off if you want. I'd say you've put in a full day." He looked into her eyes, really looked into them for the first time since Caldwell's visit. He looked at her like he wanted her to say something very specific, but before she could figure out what that was, Bermingham spoke up.

"Hey, Dani, hang on a minute, will you?"

She didn't.

He caught up with her before she made it to the steps up to Jinky's deck. If she hadn't just seen him shoving a gun into Juan's liver, she might have been more moved by the puppy-dog eyes he gave her.

"You're pissed, aren't you?"

She watched Mr. Randolph pass behind him along the path to the front of the bait shop. Bermingham didn't stand too close to her but since he stood more than a foot taller than she did, she understood the power structure at play.

"I'm a little surprised. Tucker."

"What? That's my first name. You didn't think to ask about my name." She nodded. "I didn't tell you my last name because I didn't know how much you were going to be involved in your boss's business. I wanted to know what you were like before you knew who I was. And I like to know everyone I'm doing business with."

He leaned in closer as he spoke and Dani stared into the placket of his golf shirt. The nearness of him, the size of him, convinced the secretary in her brain to line her thoughts up in a particular order.

Most people don't know what it's like to be small, especially men. To live your life at shoulder height to the majority of the population gives a person a keen sense of physical dynamics. Bermingham's suitcase probably weighed more than she did, and even with all the working out she had done, Dani knew she had few physical advantages.

But she had one.

Looking up from beneath her lashes, Dani let the corners of her mouth twist up into an almost smile. "You were afraid I'd like you for your reputation and not your boyish charms."

She saw him relax as he put his hand on the railing beside her. She wanted to duck under it and run as fast as she could. Instead she brought her fingers up and wrapped them loosely around his wrist, tracing patterns on the soft skin of his pulse point.

"And what makes you think," she whispered in a sing-song, "that I would prefer boyish charms to a bad reputation?"

"Gee," Bermingham leaned in closer, his breath warm on her face, "maybe I wanted to stand out. Your boss has a lot of bad men doing business in his bar. I plan on being a part of that in the future. Maybe I'd like to find out if I have an ally in this place. Maybe I just wanted to get the lay of the land."

Dani made herself giggle. "So to speak." Bermingham brushed his lips against hers and she shoved him playfully. "Well, you may be a big shot but I'm still a housekeeper and a bartender and I've got to hustle for my money, so spin-the-bottle is going to have to wait until my shift is done."

"I thought he just gave you the day off."

Shit. She stuck to the truth. "He did, but I've got to get my run in." She dropped the bucket on the steps and slipped under Bermingham's arm. He made no move to stop her, just smiled as she passed. "I've got to keep my ass this size. I can't afford new clothes."

"Looks like you're doing a pretty good job of it so far."

She smiled at him over her shoulder, gave her hips a little swing. As soon as she turned the corner toward the front of the bait shop, she stepped out of her flip-flops. The gravel on the path cut into her feet but she didn't flinch. She followed the path past the office, scooped up her sneakers where they sat beside her running clothes she'd left there to dry. She almost stopped to change but just pressed her feet into the shoes as she walked. As soon as her feet hit the paved road out of the fishing camp, Dani started to run.

X X X

10:51am, 99° F

Pound pound pound.

The heat made the asphalt feel mushy and Dani was distantly aware that in some spots her heels actually stuck to the melting ground. In the steady rhythm of the stride she heard two words over and over again.

Set. Up.

She didn't want to hear them. She didn't want to believe them and she wouldn't let them take root in her mind, but every step, every breath, sounded the same.

Set-up.

Tucker singling her out from all the women in the Florida Keys, all the tan girls partying at Jinky's. He smiled at her. Flirted with her. Because he had business with her boss.

Her boss had business with the FBI.

Pound. Pound. Pound.

Set-up. Set-up. Set-up.

Was she being set up? Maybe someone was using her to set someone else up. It didn't matter who and it didn't matter why. She wanted no part of it.

She saw Caldwell's smirking face and remembered her urge to run. Not down the beach, not another mile in the sand, but out of the state, out of the south. She could go to Oregon. She could go to Arizona. She could go anywhere.

And they'd find her.

Pound. Pound. Pound.

Would she have thought this a year ago? Before Rasmund, would she have felt the same panic being lied to by Tucker, being played against any of her previous bosses?

She threw herself off the center of the bridge, seeing a school of silver minnows feeding as she fell. There was only one place to swim. Mr. Randolph's dock. Her home.

Stroke. Stroke. Stroke. Breathe.

Six years ago she'd been working in a dive bar in Oklahoma. She'd slept with a Fed then. She'd slept with cops and rangers too.

She didn't give it another thought. Nobody used her any more than she used them and for nothing more important than a little sweaty fun and a break in the monotony of the everyday.

Stroke. Stroke. Stroke.

The government had used her and thrown her away.

Breathe.

She'd seen people thrown away before. She'd seen them in the bars and in truck stops. She'd seen them as a little girl on the road with her father—desperate people selling themselves, selling anything, stealing what they needed because they believed they didn't deserve anything better. Because they were garbage. They'd been used and thrown away.

Dani sensed the inlet ahead and sped up. She took a deep breath, dropped below the surface and kicked hard.

They'd thrown her mother away.

Her body cut through the water, the current at her feet, and Dani let momentum carry her before she drew her arms back to propel her.

She stopped thinking.

Her lungs ached for oxygen and her pulse pounded in her ears. Two more strong kicks, two more long sweeps of her arm, and the seaweed around Mr. Randolph's dock brushed past her shoulder, her fingers brushed the end of the rope strung from the top of the bar's deck.

No thinking. Just climbing.

Hand over hand Dani pulled herself up out of the water, the still painful ache in her shoulder feeling almost like pleasure in its familiarity. Up and up she pulled and twisted, her hands sure and rough against the slick rope.

The rough edge of the deck railing scraped her shoulder. She ignored the protests of the couple at a nearby table she dripped on. Dani knew six more pulls and she'd be at the top. She'd be above the deck and off the earth and away from anyone or anything who thought they could put their hands on her.

The wood of the deck awning felt hot against her forehead as she wound her feet in the rope to free her hands and whispered the words she whispered every day.

"You are your safe place." Slap.

"You keep yourself safe." Slap.

Dani relaxed her grip and shimmied down the rope, onto the railing, and hopped down onto the wooden deck. She wasn't quite ready to be disposed of yet.

CHAPTER TWELVE

"Interesting workout."

Choo-Choo sat on the top step of the deck staring out at the open water.

"Takes the edge off."

"Your GI Jane climb? Did it help? You didn't look like you were in the mood for company when you took off out of here."

"Do I look like I am now?"

He shrugged. "Now it would just be awkward to walk away."

Dani flopped down beside him. They both ignored the water that poured off her clothes. She knew she'd regret not changing into running clothes before taking off, her underwire bra and heavy cotton shorts rasping against her wet skin. Knowing it would just get more uncomfortable, she reached under her knit shirt and undid her bra, pulling the straps through the arm holes to free herself, and flinging the dripping lace onto the deck behind her.

"Here." He pulled his white cotton shirt over his head. Dani hesitated for just a moment, then pulled her own heavy shirt off and put on his dry one. Then she stood up enough to pull off her wet bottoms, tucking his long shirt underneath her as she sat back down. He laughed. "Not even a look to see if anyone was watching. Dani Britton, you tramp."

"You don't know the half of it." She told him about Tucker and their kiss and his true identity. She told him about their conversation after the meeting. "And so now it looks like I'm the flavor of the day for the most dangerous man in Florida. Yay me."

"What are you going to do about it?"

"What would you do?"

"I'd fuck him." When Dani said nothing to that, just stared at him, Choo-Choo shrugged again. "What did you think I was going to say? Tell you to slap his face and cry righteous chastity? This isn't some Lifetime movie. Nobody cares about your virtue. Why are you staring at me?"

Dani started to laugh. "I'm so glad you're here. It's like you're reading my mind. I keep thinking that he's only here until Friday; would you think I'm shallow if I said that he's cute too, although it's hard to keep that in mind when everyone around you is petrified of him."

"And that terror is another excellent reason to be accommodating. If not the best reason."

She rested her chin on her knees. "And let's face it. I've done worse."

"Haven't we all?"

She looked over her shoulder at him, seeing the network of scars that exploded across his chest and stomach. Leaning back, she let her finger drift over his skin, over the jagged line of a long scar that ran from beneath his left arm to his sternum, where it took a sharp turn toward his belly. Smaller white scars radiated out and down across his body. He didn't flinch.

"Wow."

"Yeah." He leaned forward to show her the long, straight scar that ran along his spine.

"You know, those scars could be good for some drinks around here." She bumped her knee against his. "Every time someone asks me about mine—which doesn't happen often, you'll be glad to hear—I make up another story and Mr. Randolph buys everyone in the bar a drink. I think we're up to twenty-three rounds now."

"Twenty-three, huh? That's a lot of stories to come up with."

"None of them are more far-fetched than the truth."

Choo-Choo nodded and then squinted at her. "So would I be number twenty-four or would I start new with my own list?"

"Hmm." Dani shrugged. "I think that's up to Rolly in the kitchen. He keeps track."

He ran his fingers over one of the smaller scars. "It'd be nice to have something to show for these."

She shook her head at the damage to his skin. "At least we know our government isn't wasting taxpayers' money on plastic surgeons."

"Yeah," he said again, his voice soft. Dani saw his mouth tighten the way it had when she'd sat with him at the airport, like he was struggling to spit words out or keep them in. She let him take his time. "I don't mind them. The scars. Does that sound weird?"

"I'm probably not the best judge of that."

He almost laughed at that, staring out over the water. Dani had to lean close to hear him. "I was seven when I was sent away to school the first time. My father was supposed to take a post in the UK so they put me in this boarding school in Wales that my brothers had gone to. Then it turned out he took a post in Singapore instead."

Choo-Choo shifted on the dock, his leg pressed against hers. "My mother said it would be too unsettling to transfer me from the school in the middle of the year. I'd been there two weeks. I was seven." He kept staring at some point on the horizon. "I was little for my age. Pretty." He let the word sit there for a long moment before shaking his head, as if dismissing the thought. "Perhaps this isn't the time for my sexual Dickensian tale of woe."

"Thank God. My well of woe is pretty full right now."

"My point is, Dani, we've all been told there's this happy-happy lifestyle everyone is leading, that there's this idyllic childhood and super-wholesome family plan that we're all supposed to yearn for, but you know what? It's like black holes or electrons. There's no proof. I've never seen it with my own eyes. Did you see any proof of it in Flat Road, Oklahoma?"

She shook her head.

"No, me neither. I went from school to school and eventually from bed to bed because that's where I had to be. That's what I had to do and I learned to make it work for me. I used it to my advantage. Hell, I was good at it; I made it an art form. And now? My spectacular fall from grace put me back on top of the darling list this summer, but every time someone decided to put their hands on me when I didn't want it—and sometimes even when I did—I'd strip off my shirt and show them these beauties."

He fingered the long scar on his sternum. "They're hideous and I love them. They're like my own personal 'Keep Out' sign. I'd watch people try to hide their distaste, trying to decide if I was worth it."

Dani watched his long fingers move over his skin. "So you're going celibate and telling me to bang the bad guy?"

"I said nothing about celibacy." He turned to her, leaning down to look her in the eye. "I'm talking about changing the rules of the game, taking control of the field. All these pedestrian notions about morality and dignity are just fairy tales. Here's the reality. You do what you have to do until you don't have to do it anymore."

After a long moment she looked away and down where his hand rested on her gunshot scar. "You and I should get a tattoo of that shit."

He snorted and she began to giggle. Their laughter blew away on the tidal breeze.

X X X

11:58am, 103° F

Oren poured himself a vodka and watched Bermingham, who stood in the doorway to the deck, his back to the bar. Oren watched Bermingham watch the two figures laughing and talking on the stairs.

He hoped to get a glimpse of Bermingham unguarded. He didn't know what he wanted to see there—jealousy, irritation, hurt feelings—just something that would crack the irritatingly cheerful college-boy façade he wore outside of that meeting room. The events of the past two days conspired to make Oren feel old. Not just old, either, but passé. What happened to bad guys looking like bad guys? The Wheelers managed it. They didn't have the polished flash Oren remembered from his heavy coke days, but their speed-wild eyes and their twitchy mannerisms made it easy for a savvy person to know what side of the law they operated on.

Golf shirts and dimples?

It sat wrong with Oren, like sneaking drugs inside of baby dolls. Some realities shouldn't mix. He had to give it to the Canadian, however. The gee-shucks act contrasted nicely with the icy power he wielded. It was disarming.

Had it disarmed Dani?

Or had Dani disarmed Oren?

The questions made his head hurt. This wasn't what he signed on for. He hadn't worked so hard to kick his habit and save his dimes only so he could find himself caught between two sides of a new generation of psychopaths. He didn't mind a little bit of gray business. He didn't even mind if the business deals got shadier than gray, as long as he could walk away from them. But the drugs had gotten heavier and the weapons had gotten bigger and if the deals started involving explosives or, God forbid, something even more deadly, he wanted no part of it.

He made a decision. Once this deal with Bermingham was finished, Oren planned to cut all ties with the Wheelers. They needed his dock and his connections, and they could use them both, this one last time. Juan would be pissed if he shut it down, but when wasn't he? If this deal was as big as both sides seemed to think it was, Oren could use it as his ticket out of this life on the edges of the underworld.

In the meantime, he had a bar to run.

Speaking of which, Peg had left a note that someone wanted to reserve a room for the month. If they dealt with Peg on the phone and still wanted to rent, they were the kind of person Oren wanted to do business with. Everybody needed to chill the hell out. This was Redemption Key, for God's sake, not New York City.

Bermingham strolled up to the bar, whatever he'd been dwelling on while watching Dani now tucked away under his floppy hair and goofy smile. Oren couldn't get over just how big the guy was. Big in that kind of way you didn't realize until you were being dwarfed by him. On a good day Oren flirted with six feet; the Canadian had to be at least five inches over that and broad enough across the beam that everything seemed in proportion. Up close, with sweat pressing his golf shirt against his chest, the guy looked as solid as a redwood.

Imagine what he must look like to someone Dani's size.

Oren hoped he hid his shiver.

"You ever get used to these gorgeous sunrises and sunsets, Randolph?" Bermingham climbed onto a barstool.

"I never take one for granted, if that's what you're asking."

The Canadian grinned. At least his mouth did. His eyes did something hard that made Oren's stomach clench. "That's probably a good way to live. Never assume there's going to be another one, eh?" Then the frat boy face came fully back online. "I could get used to living like this. I could call this place home."

"Let me get you a beer." Oren bent down into the cooler, keeping the end of that sentence to himself. *And shove it up your Canadian ass.*

X X X

12:40pm, 104° F

Dani came up the front steps by the bait shop to the kitchen door. She figured Bermingham would be on the premises somewhere and hoped she'd get a chance to see Mr. Randolph first.

Rolly wolf-whistled and Dani gave him a little bow. Choo-Choo suggested she wear something appropriately skimpy to keep Bermingham happy. The closest thing she had was a black cotton slip dress. The spaghetti straps showed off her shoulder scars but Choo-Choo assured her that the way the fabric clung to her ass, nobody would be looking at her shoulders. She remembered why she rarely wore the dress.

Mr. Randolph's voice made her jump. "Don't you look like a party waiting to happen?"

She hoped her tan hid most of her blush. And she really wished she'd worn a bra. Standing in the middle of Jinky's kitchen, Dani suddenly felt obvious.

"Mr. Randolph." She stepped closer, half expecting him to step away. She didn't think Rolly would care about their conversation— and there really were no secrets in Jinky's—but this felt like a confession. "I didn't know who he was. Bermingham. I really didn't. I wouldn't . . ."

Mr. Randolph nodded, staring over her head out the door, not really looking at anything, it seemed. Just not looking at her. "Okay, Dani. It happens. But now you know who he is. You know what he is." He finally looked at her, over her clothes with a look that made her want to grab a towel. "You do what you need to do. Maybe this will work out for all of us. Maybe you'll keep him happy enough that he won't shoot any of us through the head."

He started to pat her on the shoulder the way he always did but caught himself, cutting the gesture off early and moving past her to the door. Dani could see Rolly listening in, pointedly keeping his face down over the cutting board. So much for being discreet.

"I know you have plans tonight." Mr. Randolph paused with the screen door open. "But I need you to get some rooms ready. Mr. Bermingham is going to be our guest until his business is finished and, surprises of surprises, we actually have a paying customer coming in tonight. See if you can find the time to get a room ready, all right? Oh, and get Bermingham another beer."

He didn't wait for her answer.

X X X

12:40pm, 104° F

Booker turned off the highway at the Walgreens. Marlene at the rental car desk in the airport at Key West couldn't have been nicer, drawing him a little map on the back of the rental contract. She and her husband, Mitch, used to fish at Jinky's, and she assured him that after the craziness of Key West, Redemption would feel like heaven. She recommended getting pizza at someplace called No Name Pub and advised him to keep a sharp eye out for Key deer.

"For an endangered species," she'd whispered, "they are everywhere!"

Booker had listened and laughed, following her directions as she scribbled them. He smiled and nodded but he wasn't really hearing her. His mind pulled him elsewhere. He wanted off this island. He didn't like islands.

He didn't mind the heat; he thought the houses and boats beautiful in their way. Traffic moved smoothly but Tom Booker had never been able to relax anywhere that had only one way out. One road moved everyone into and out of the Keys. He could in theory take a boat, but he didn't exactly have one handy. He had a rental car and only one road to drive it on.

When he drove through Big Pine, he realized he was heading to an island that didn't even have a through road. Redemption Key was a dead end.

Booker pulled the little car under a sign for something called THE LADY OF SPAIN PARTY PONTOON. A half-dozen cars were parked across the pitted lot. Nobody would notice one more.

Marlene had told him it was less than a mile from here to the bridge onto Redemption. Less than a mile wasn't too far to walk, especially if it meant having an unblockable exit.

He turned the car around so it faced out of the lot toward the road, calculating the best angle for a quick departure if needed. He dropped his keys into the pocket behind the passenger's seat and saw his bags.

He couldn't check into a hotel—or fishing camp, whatever that was—without luggage. The bag didn't weigh anything. Carrying it was no problem, and there was nothing in it to identify him if he had to leave it behind. But he didn't know what to do with the yarn bag. He'd finished the afghan on the flight. The afghan he'd made for Dani.

What had he been thinking?

For one thing, it was hot, almost one hundred degrees. Who needed an afghan in this weather? For another thing, he'd been hired to kill Dani before, and she'd gotten away, damn near killing him in the process. Was a gift appropriate?

He wasn't sure how he felt about any of this.

He could always come back and get it if things worked out.

That decided, Booker climbed from the car, oblivious to the heat that hammered down on him. He reached into the backseat, tucking the yarn bag down into the floor well and pulling his suitcase out.

He almost locked the door, catching it just before it shut. He laughed at his absentmindedness. He needed to get his act together.

He needed to remember where he left the car, to pay attention to how many steps and in what direction he'd need to make it back to this spot. No streetlights, he noted. It would be pitch-black at night, he'd bet.

And he needed to find a bait shop or hardware store. Booker felt naked without his knives.

CHAPTER THIRTEEN

12:50pm, 104° F

Dani brought Bermingham another Corona.

He shook his head and winked at her as he took the bottle. "You've really got to get better taste in beer. This is like water."

"It's a good beer in the heat."

Bermingham's face brightened at that. "Really? Never thought of that. Maybe I should work on getting a taste for it since it looks like I might be doing a little more business down here. Speaking of which, your boss is picking up the tab for my room. That's really generous of him."

"Mr. Randolph is a very generous man."

"I'm looking forward to doing business with him." Dani noticed that Bermingham had yet to look anywhere but her face, his gaze never checking out her body in the slight dress. She didn't quite know what to make of that.

"Where's your buddy?"

"Ned? He's making some last-minute arrangements. This deal is taking longer than it should." Bermingham didn't look angry. He looked distracted, glancing at his phone.

She hopped up on the bar and swung her legs over the front, beside him. She wanted it to look flirtatious. She wanted a peek at his phone. "Is your room okay?"

"Yeah, it's good." He didn't look up. "Hot though. This fucking heat."

"You get used to it." He made a sound of doubt. "Waiting for a call?"

"Picture from the Wheelers of the product." He chewed on the inside of his mouth, ignoring her as she swung her feet near his side. When his phone beeped, he leaned back, keeping her from seeing it, and stared at the screen for several seconds, his expression dark.

"Bad news? Did it melt or something?"

"What? No." He closed the picture and looked at her closely. "Melting isn't really the thing we've got to worry about."

"Oh." She shrugged, knowing he was searching her face for something. She hopped off the bar and turned away from him. "Well, I have to go set up the other room. I guess I'll—"

Bermingham was up and on her before she could finish, his hand gripping her arm tightly enough to get her on her toes and just shy enough of bruising.

"What other room?"

Dani didn't have to feign fear. Tucker Bermingham had over a foot on her and his hand span covered most of her upper arm. Even bent down into her face the way he was, she had to struggle to stay on tiptoe to keep her shoulder from being wrenched.

"The other room. Someone's renting another room. Mr. Randolph told me to—"

"Who is renting the other room?"

"I don't know!" She let her eyes go wide, putting on a face she hoped looked as defenseless as she felt. "It's a hotel. A fishing camp. It's what we do. People rent rooms."

Bermingham swore and dropped her arm. The gap between letting her go and apologizing took less than a second, but Dani saw it. She saw the gears switching in his expression.

"Sorry, Dani. I didn't mean to scare you." He rubbed her arm and Dani resisted the urge to back away. That long, lanky awkwardness she had found so adorable in the bar just hours ago had disappeared, and she was all too aware of the physical power in the man before her.

"I should go."

"Wait." He closed his eyes and sighed. "Wait. I'm sorry." There was that smile again, dimples and all. He carded his fingers through his hair; Dani noticed how he managed to get it to flop just so over his eyes as he grinned sheepishly. "I'm being a jerk. I've got a lot on my mind and this deal is a really big thing. But that's no excuse to be rude to you. Here I've got a beautiful girl all alone in a bar and I'm being a jerk. I'm really sorry."

Dani made a show of hiding a smile she didn't feel, pushing at Bermingham's hard chest with both hands. "You are a jerk. I put this dress on for you and you haven't even looked at me."

"Oh I've looked at you." He trailed his fingers down her arms and probably would have raised goose bumps if her elbow didn't still throb from his squeeze. "I keep on looking at you, Dani Britton. And I keep asking myself why a cute girl like you spends her time in a place like this? What's in it for you?"

"The glamour?" His laugh sounded genuine and, against her natural instinct, Dani stepped in a little closer. "And I get to meet interesting people sometimes."

"That must be easy for a friendly girl like you."

"You're not very observant."

"But I bet you are."

The speed with which he answered her put her on alert. "Why do I suspect you're going to ask a favor of me?"

"Because you're smart?" Dimples. "And because maybe you'd like to see more of me in the future. Look, I really need this deal to go off smoothly. I really, really need the Wheelers to come through for me."

"You really need your twenty-five prime units."

"You were listening."

Dani let out a low laugh. "You were kind of hard to ignore earlier, what with shoving Juan's gun into his liver. What is it that they're bringing you? That has to stay so cool?"

He ran his fingers across her shoulder, up into her hairline. Dani leaned into his palm, letting him tilt her face up toward his. "Your boss didn't tell you?"

"My boss doesn't know." She saw his smirk. "He tries to stay out of the Wheelers' business as much as possible. Everyone does."

"And yet, here we are, getting ready to make the deal."

"The Wheelers can be very convincing. Not everyone has the ability or the nerve to body slam Juan Wheeler."

"Well I do." His fingers tangled in her hair as he pressed her against him. She had to keep her head back, her chin against his chest, to look him in the face. His hands were gentle against her and she slid her arms around his waist. It felt like hugging a tree—a warm, muscular, terrible tree. When he spoke, she could feel the words in the muscles of his back. "That's why it's good that we're getting along so well."

"That sounds mildly scary."

"This whole situation could get scary fast. I can keep you safe and I will but I need something from you."

She smiled up at him to hide her nerves. "Something besides low thread count sheets?"

The way he stared into her eyes made her feel like she was right back in that hospital in DC, hooked up to IV drips, being grilled by everyone in the country who had a badge. He was taking her measure and not even trying to hide it. Dani let her thoughts line up in their own particular order, dragging the fear and anger off to a private corner of her mind.

Let him stare.

He smiled. Finally. "I need you to pay attention to what your boss is doing. And his friends. Do you know his friends? Someone named Caldwell?"

That was unexpected.

"I know who you mean."

He nodded. "Word is he and your boss are good friends."

"And?"

He splayed his long fingers against the small of her back. In any other situation it would have felt seductive. "And are we going to pretend that neither one of us knows what he does for a living?"

Dani shook her head, her mouth too dry to speak.

"Good." He leaned in and brushed his face against hers. "I want to keep you safe, Dani, but this deal is going down. Nothing can keep this from happening. Do you hear what I'm saying? So it would really be helpful to me if you would keep your eyes and ears open for me. Your boss is more involved in this deal than he's letting on and I just want to make sure that everyone sticks to the arrangement." His hand slid softly under her chin. That her jaw fit easily into the palm of his hand wasn't lost on Dani.

"I'm calling the shots here now, Dani. Not your boss. Not Vincente. Not those moron Wheeler boys. Everyone answers to me now. I've got to know. Can I trust you?"

A yes wasn't going to cut it.

Dani slid her small hands up the expanse of his chest until they met behind his neck and she pulled him down to her. Even moving with her, it felt like dragging iron, and Dani let him lift her off the floor into his embrace. The kiss deepened and she felt that same breathlessness she'd felt with Bermingham on the porch. She let herself drift in it.

There was a part of her brain for things like this too.

Bermingham seemed reassured and convinced when they pulled apart. He slipped his fingers through hers when she stepped back, begging off to finish setting up the other room. He teasingly grilled her about going to meet another man and Dani answered with mock mystery.

She really hoped the pleasure center of her brain would hold the foreground of her mind long enough for her to get out of the bar without screaming.

X X X

Dani exhaled slowly as she headed down to the office to grab a room key and the key to the linen closet to set up the room for the new guest. Mr. Randolph or Peg, whoever had taken the reservation, had set the key out for her as they had dozens of times since she'd taken this job. At this moment, everything and everyone felt threatening to her. She struggled to remember the way it felt when this was her only job, when the biggest irritation was a broken air-conditioner and the only thing she was scared of was facing a pissed-off rat.

Bermingham knew Caldwell was FBI.

And he thought Mr. Randolph was trying something shifty.

Mr. Randolph was openly terrified of the Wheelers and the Wheelers were terrified of Bermingham and now Bermingham was getting nervous. Nerves make dangerous people more dangerous. How much more dangerous could this situation get?

X X X

1:15pm, 104° F

Booker climbed onto the oak barstool and hooked his feet over the lower rung. He rolled his shoulders, letting the heat soak into his muscles, loosening them from the walk. He could have gone right to his room. The leathery woman behind the bar had tossed him a key and shrugged in a general direction after swiping his fake credit card, but Booker wanted to sit for a minute. He wanted to get a feel for the place.

Jinky's.

By the name he'd expected some sort of '50s-style soda shop, not this rough, bare-floored gin joint. He scanned the walls and ceilings. Every inch of every surface was covered in pictures and postcards and license plates and pieces of underwear, stapled, nailed, taped, skewered, and otherwise attached in what looked like a decades-old patina of debauchery. It felt authentic in a way that newer bars could never hope to achieve.

It wasn't anything he would have chosen for himself—Booker didn't drink—but he could appreciate the view out over the inlet and the general sense of Floridian ease. But he hadn't traveled all this way for either of those things.

He was here for Dani.

He tensed at the shiver that coursed through him. He'd been feeling them all day. They'd been shimmying underneath his skin since he'd manipulated Agent Davis into searching for Dani's file. Booker had done all he could to keep thoughts of Dani hidden deep within himself. His new employers had asked about his feelings toward her and he thought he'd been pretty successful convincing them she'd just been another target.

Of course, his new employers were stupid in a lot of ways.

They lacked any originality of feeling and couldn't have collected a splinter's worth of imagination among the lot of them. He was glad for it because the last thing Booker wanted to do was discuss his complicated feelings toward Dani Britton with some cold-blooded therapist.

He didn't know how he felt.

That understanding alone added an element of excitement to his anticipation.

He'd been hired to kill Dani and she'd proven a fascinating target. Adorable and underestimated and clever and tough. She'd gotten away from him, damn near killed him.

He didn't know how he felt about that either.

There weren't many situations Booker went into with so little certainty. This one made his fingertips tingle. He sipped his ginger ale and watched the sun bake the deck outside.

XXX

2:00pm, 104° F

Out of habit, Dani grabbed the bucket and towel hanging off the side of the deck and began bussing tables. She felt separate from the scene around her. She'd fallen in love with this island at night. At night everything was soft—the warm, moist air, the breeze off the water, the light from the moon. People spoke more softly and Peg kept the reggae low through the speakers. At night she often sat on the railing, listening to Mr. Randolph entertain tourists, watching stars come out, and thinking of nothing.

Nights like that were far away now.

But there wasn't anything she could do about it. The Wheelers were on their way with their shipment of God only knew what. Sunset was hours away. Choo-Choo was off talking to Casper about a job and Mr. Randolph, well, she didn't want to think of Mr. Randolph right now. She didn't want to spy on him for Bermingham and she didn't want to see the way he looked at her, thinking she was already guilty of it.

By dawn, the deal would go down and nothing would be the same again. Maybe she'd wind up working for Bermingham and have to say good-bye to Mr. Randolph. Maybe the Wheelers would start blowing people away. Maybe the Feds would crash everything. She didn't know much about this Vincente character but what she had learned didn't suggest he'd add much sunshine to any of the above. She might as well save the thinking for another time. She had cash; she had a car. Hopefully she wouldn't get shot again. Funny the things a person can get used to.

Without the *Lady of Spain*, it wasn't as crowded inside as yesterday. Dani could just make out the faces in the shadows after squinting into the brilliant sunshine. One of the Australians slumped unconscious at a corner table, abandoned by his friends when they'd headed out to snorkel. Angel Jackson played dominoes with one of the fishing boat captains. Peg checked her phone by the window to the kitchen, ignoring the couple making out in the center of the bar and a lone guy at the far end. Dani slung the bucket under the bar's flip-up gate and ducked underneath it. Peg ignored her too as she dumped bottles into the garbage and moved on to put the glasses into the sink. The couple kept making out with a lot more tongue than Dani would have thought absolutely necessary, so Dani looked away toward the far end of the bar.

And saw blue eyes.

It was too dark to see the color but Dani knew exactly how blue those eyes were. She knew the shape of his head, the curl of his black hair and where it would fall over his pale forehead. She knew what the smile would look like.

All she could think was, "Boy, it's not like it is in the movies."

If this were a movie, she'd scream or faint or at least drop the bucket. She'd reel. He'd sneer and one of them would say a line worthy of the coming attractions.

None of that happened.

Dani felt that all-too-familiar sensation of her thoughts scattering, fleeing to the edges of consciousness to decide who would handle the scene before her.

Tom Booker sat less than ten feet from her, looking exactly as he had when he'd tried to kill her, exactly as he had in every dream she'd had since being pulled from the Tidal Basin, shot and broken and terrified.

No. Not exactly. He looked kind of shocked.

It would have taken a much more naïve person than she to think his presence here was coincidence. But he looked shocked, uneasy. Dani stood still, the fact-checker in her brain trying to pin down what that expression was.

He looked nervous. Imagine that. Tom Booker, the man who orchestrated the murder of all of her coworkers, the man who had pursued her relentlessly one icy night in November, who had tried to gut her with a knife while still handling her with that terrible tenderness—that man looked nervous to see her. Huh.

His tongue flickered across his chapped lips.

"Hello, Dani."

The voice did it. The sound of her name in his voice snapped her from the fugue of disbelief. That reeling she'd wondered about smashed into her and if she hadn't already had a hand on the metal bar sink, she'd have stumbled against it. She didn't think she'd moved—she didn't know if she could—but every fiber in Dani's body wanted to throw her head back and let out a howl of primal rage.

Instead she said, "Hi, Tom."

And there was that smile. She stepped closer, thoughts of a mongoose and a cobra flickering somewhere in her head, although she couldn't remember which one hunted which. She stepped closer and could see her memory had been correct. His eyes were still the blue she remembered, still strangely beautiful.

In one step she calculated how quickly he could reach her and snap her neck and how hard she would have to swing the bucket to smash his face and how sorry she was that the bucket was plastic and not metal and how useless it would probably be and how strange it was the men she found attractive.

She thought how far the universe had gone to prove to her that she could never get away.

It kind of seemed like overkill.

She got it. There wasn't a safe place on this planet.

CHAPTER FOURTEEN

2:00pm, 104° F

Oren slid the screen door closed behind him and dropped into the chaise lounge on his porch. His house looked out over the open water, the inlet to the right on the other side of the thick hedge of sea grape. At night, if he tilted his head just right he could hear soft music coming from the deck of the bar on the other side of the hedge. If trouble broke out, he'd be able to hear it without tilting his head. That was as far as Oren went with security systems.

Not that they would have helped him today.

After tomorrow, Jinky's was going to hell. He knew that with the certainty of a man whose drug habit had kept him circling the pit for too many years. There was only so long a man could bump shoulders with darkness before stepping all the way through. He should have put his foot down with the Wheelers years ago. He should have faced them down before they'd taken over the local underworld the way they had. They hadn't always been as dangerous as they were now. Sure, they'd always been batshit crazy and armed to the teeth, but by avoiding the ugliness, he'd let them gain inches that turned into miles that turned into a road that ran smack-dab into the middle of his life.

And Bermingham had found that road and ridden right in on it.

That was the problem with predators. There was always another bigger, scarier, more persistent predator right behind them. And people like Oren were just side dishes to the main meal.

When he heard careful footsteps crunching the gravel beside the house, Oren fully expected to see Bermingham or his thug emerge from the shadows, gun in hand, to end his life. As a testimony to his train of thought—and to the vodka—the thought didn't make him panic. It just made him tired.

Caldwell crept onto the porch, pulling the screen door closed silently. When Oren sat up, the agent put his finger to his lips and tipped his head in the direction of Oren's living room. Oren followed his friend inside, sliding the inside door shut, not saying a word as Caldwell moved to the stereo system on the far wall. In seconds, guitar music flooded the room, louder than Oren usually played it.

Caldwell stepped very close and grabbed his arm. Oren kept his voice just above a whisper. "I never thought I'd say this, buddy, but I sure hope you're getting ready to kiss me."

"I wish," the agent hissed. "But I think it's likely we're both getting ready to get fucked. Have you noticed anything rearranged in here? Anyone on the premises that shouldn't be?"

"You're kidding, right? Nobody's had a key to this door since Carter was in the White House. As for the bar, half the regulars there probably have warrants out. What is this?"

Caldwell sighed. "I just had a very unpleasant phone call from my superior after I ran a check on your girl."

"You already ran a check on Dani."

"Yeah," he said. "I ran it on Dani and got nothing. I ran it together with her friend, blondie. Turns out Choo-Choo is a Charbaneaux, something of a society celebrity, and running a check on any Charbaneaux is bad news; running it together with one Danielle Britton gets my dick slammed in a drawer. Come on; let's get away from the window.

Oren followed him to the little breakfast bar that marked off the kitchen. Caldwell knew his way around as well as Oren and pulled the vodka from the freezer. Neither bothered with ice.

XXX

2:00pm, 104° F

Booker didn't think he'd be able to speak. He rarely felt the air temperature around him, was only aware of it in a passing way, so the heat he felt moving through his muscles unsettled him. This wasn't how he had expected to feel. It certainly wasn't how he had expected Dani to react.

He'd expected rage, fear, tears. Staring into her soft brown eyes, though, Booker realized how stupid that expectation was. This was Dani Britton. She always surprised him.

How cute she looked. More than cute. He'd known she was tiny; he'd been in her closet, seen her little shoes. But he'd met her in November when she'd been bundled up in layers upon layers of woolly shirts. She didn't wear those layers now.

She didn't wear much at all.

He wanted to let his eyes roam over the tan expanse of her little arms. He wouldn't have imagined her to be so toned. Or so dark. Of course they had met in November, winter, miles from the equator, months ago. It felt like only days had passed.

She was still his Dani. She still met his gaze with that calm, easy stare. She wasn't hiding behind bundles of clothes and bags now. She wasn't hiding at all, and as much as he wanted to let his eyes take in the smooth shoulders and to follow the seam of the little dress where it headed south, he didn't want it to be like that. He didn't want to ogle her.

"Hi, Tom."

Another shiver rushed beneath his skin. Her voice. He thought he remembered everything about Dani Britton; he'd replayed their phone calls over and over in his head. He remembered the unhidden fear in her voice, the way she'd listened to him and talked to him—really talked to him. He thought he remembered everything, but nothing prepared him for the sound of her voice again, face-to-face.

"Did you come to kill me?"

He laughed out loud. That was his Dani, getting right to the point.

"I don't think so." It was a strange way to answer. It just popped out. "I've never been to Florida before. I was surprised to find out you were here. It's a long way from Oklahoma. And DC."

"Not far enough, apparently."

She said it with a little smile and Booker felt another rush of heat.

"I've been thinking about you."

Then she laughed. "I've been thinking about you too."

Booker wasn't so far out of the stream of human interaction that he didn't catch the edge in her tone. Was this a mistake? Should he have kept his presence a secret, watched Dani in private for a while? This wasn't like him. He didn't stammer and blush like a schoolboy.

But then, he didn't get to meet girls like Dani.

Except when he was hired to kill them, and that was a different story.

Dani sighed and swung the bucket she carried into the deep bar sink. When she reached forward to turn on the faucet, he saw the starburst of scars across her shoulder. He didn't think. Before he knew it he stood on the rungs of the stool, stretching long across the bar to put his fingertips on the jagged white lines. When his fingertips touched her warm skin, he felt her jump, her muscles twitching along her back.

X X X

2:08pm, 104° F

It was only the crack of a metal bolt against her knee that shocked Dani enough to keep her from leaping onto the counter. She wouldn't have screamed. She couldn't have. Her throat had closed to the point of suffocating her.

Some part of her, some insane part of her mind that had had enough of the adrenaline and the suspense, had made her turn her back on Tom. It had wanted him to touch her, had wanted him to lunge and do whatever it was he planned on doing. It was the same part that wanted Bermingham's shipment to show up, wanted dawn to get here and to find out once again if she was going to get shot or strangled or have to run for her life.

"What happened?" His voice was reverent as his fingertips traced the knotty scars.

She didn't turn around. She didn't think about what his fingers felt like.

"What do you think happened? Don't you remember?"

"I remember you going over. I hit my head pretty hard."

At that she turned, stepping close to the bar, following him as he dropped back on the stool. "You hit your head pretty hard?" She spit out the words as she climbed on a shelf, lifting herself so she bent over the bar into his face. "Let me see."

He didn't back away from her, but his eyes widened. "What?"

"Let me see where you hit your head. Let me see the scars."

"There are no scars." He ran his fingers over his cheekbone and around his eye. "This was all rebuilt. They did it from the inside so there wouldn't be any scars."

She was close enough to bite him. "Well that was awfully nice of them."

Could he see how much she wanted to bite him? To give him a scar? Was he afraid of her? This time he didn't have a knife; she didn't have a bullet wound in her leg. This was her territory and she felt stronger than she'd ever felt in her life. Did he see that? Is that why he seemed to tremble when she moved closer to him?

Or was it something else?

Something wet and cold bounced off the back of her neck and Dani spun around back onto the ground. Down by the kitchen Peg made a show of drying her hands on her shorts, flickering her glance up toward the deck door. Dani looked that way too in time to see the enormous figure of Bermingham walking hard and fast across the floor.

He didn't even pretend to greet her. Instead he stood right at the corner of the bar, staring squarely at Tom. He leaned forward, thick forearms sprawled on the bar, long fingers nearly reaching Tom's drink, staring into Tom's profile.

"Everything okay here?"

"Everything's fine," Dani said. "There's—"

He shot out a finger and wagged it in her face. "I'm not talking to you." Dani flinched. Bermingham hadn't looked to see how close his hand had come. Tom had seen it. He watched it as Bermingham brought it to point at him. "I'm talking to you, friend."

All that nervousness or whatever she had seen in Tom's body language disappeared under a subtle settling of his shoulders. The change came on so smoothly she almost laughed. Talking with her made him nervous. Being cornered by a man the size of Bermingham put him at ease. There was absolutely no upside to this situation.

Unless they killed each other.

Dani stepped back against the bar sink and folded her arms.

"I noticed the way you decided to reach across the bar to touch my girl. I noticed she didn't like it much. I wonder if you'd mind not doing that again."

Tom said nothing, just looked over at Dani with a little smile Bermingham couldn't miss.

"Oh. Oh. Unless . . ." The Canadian had turned back to her. He stood straight, his huge hands gripping the edge of the bar. "Is this another friend? You've got a lot of friends, Dani."

She didn't look at Tom. "He's no friend of mine."

"I'm a paying customer," Tom said.

Tom drummed his fingers on the bar before turning to smile up at the Canadian. Tom wasn't a big man. Though sinewy, he looked downright slight next to the gangster. Bermingham had at least six or seven inches on him. He had a bad temper and a worse reputation, but Dani knew—and not from hearsay—what Tom was capable of. Seeing him move so slowly, that little smile on his full lips, brought her nightmares to life in full color.

Bermingham didn't see it. He turned to Dani. "You all right? You want me to stick around? Get rid of this guy?"

Now there was a question.

Tom wiped his fingers on his drink napkin and slid from the stool. Bermingham leaned on an elbow and watched him.

"I assure you," Tom said, "there's no need to get territorial. If you'll just point me to the restrooms, I'll freshen up and then settle my bill." Bermingham pointed and Tom walked off, smiling.

"You okay?" he asked her once the men's room door had closed. "This really isn't the time to be making new friends, Dani. I don't like strangers around during a deal. Understand?"

She didn't answer him. She didn't hear him. All she could focus on was the wrinkled bar napkin Tom had dropped, and the metal Jinky's key beneath it.

X X X

2:18pm, 105° F

Caldwell finished his drink in one pull and poured another.

Oren found it difficult to swallow. "Are you going to tell me what's up?"

"I think I'm being set up. And I think they're using you to do it."

"Who?"

"The Bureau."

Oren forced down his vodka. "You're being set up by the FBI? For what?"

"I don't know. I don't know." He rolled the glass across his palm, staring at the vodka. "This is all too tidy. Bermingham, whatever the hell the Wheelers are moving that brought him all the way down from Canada, your girl showing up and getting cozy. I know you think I'm being paranoid about her connection to Bermingham, but—"

Oren cleared his throat. "I'm not so sure you are paranoid. They know each other. Dani says it just happened, that she didn't know who he was. She's pretty convincing. But if you have something that says otherwise, I'd like to hear it."

"Shit." Caldwell fumbled his drink, his fingers trembling. "Shit."

"You're going to have to do a little better than that, man. What did you find out?"

"Nothing. Absolutely nothing. I ran Dani's name and got squat. I ran the kid's name. Got nothing but society gossip. You know what else I got?" He poured again. "I got a visit. From my SAC. Not a phone call. Not from my SSA. My SAC paid me a visit in person."

"Am I supposed to know what that means?"

"It means God himself stepped down from heaven to check my emails. Special Agent in Charge Tomblin Richter doesn't make office calls. He's my boss's boss's boss. He's the Jesus of Miami. He tells the hurricanes when they can roll in. Do you hear me? He 'stopped by' my office for a little chat. With me."

"What did he say?"

"He asked what my interest was in Danielle Britton."

The look on the agent's face made that sentence far scarier than Oren thought it should be. "And what did you say?"

"I lied out my ass. Said someone had recommended I talk with her about a case I'm on. I had to stand there pretending this was

149

situation normal as he asked me if I'd found anything and then told me it was probably for the best that I hadn't."

Considering the fact that he had a six-foot-five mountain of dangerous Canadian less than two hundred feet away in his units, Oren found it difficult to see the danger in Caldwell's interoffice crisis. It must have shown on his face because Caldwell started explaining.

"Look, if I step out of line, my SSA will call me in, the Supervisory Special Agent. It happens all the time. She's my boss. If it gets serious, like the time I had to explain about Bancroft and all those diamonds—you remember that?—I get called down by the ASAC, the Assistant Special Agent in Charge. That's bad. That got me suspended, remember?"

"Yeah, of course I do. You drank a month's worth of profit that week."

"Yeah, being dressed down by the ASAC is not a good time."

"And so," Oren struggled to follow, "being called by the SAC, not his assistant, means you're in bigger trouble? For looking up a file that has nothing on it?"

Caldwell rubbed his eyes. "You're missing the point of all this. It's not just a matter of who dressed me down, it's why. If Dani has no file with us, if there's nothing to report, how did they know I was looking for her? Why does the highest-ranking agent in Miami care that I looked into a woman who has absolutely nothing on file?"

Oren couldn't think of a good way this could go. "Because . . ."

The agent nodded. "Because she has a file. And whatever is on it is important enough and dangerous enough to restrict it. And whoever is restricting it is powerful enough to have the top man in my division find me and tell me to drop it. Whoever they are, they can make my SAC their errand boy. Now you've got a girl in your bar who has that kind of juice in her past and she's on hand when one of the most wanted men in North America just happens to be doing a deal so big that the fucking Wheelers are squealing? You tell me that my bosses haven't put two and two together and come up with a big fat implication for you? And if you're implicated and I'm sitting on my ass at your bar not blowing the whistle, I'm implicated. You see what I'm saying?"

"Oh shit. I suddenly feel a strong urge to sail to Cuba."

"Yeah, well, if the Wheelers have decided to step up their game and move into weapons, especially weapons that could be used in domestic terrorism, you and I might be going to Cuba sooner than you think. We might get to be bunkmates at Gitmo."

"Tell me you're working on worst-case scenarios there."

"Can you think of a reason not to?" Caldwell leaned back against the counter. He looked exhausted. "I might be totally wrong. I may have this all wrong from the get-go, but you've got to admit there is something rotten here. Something is not adding up. There are too many strangers without enough information. No matter how I look at it, no matter who comes into play, all eyes seem to keep turning back to your girl and I want to know why."

"Can't you go to your superiors and tell them about the deal with Bermingham going down tomorrow? Can't you say you got a tip? Surely to God you're not still trying to protect me and Jinky's. The last thing I'm worried about at this point is having the law around."

"I've told them. I told my supervisor and she told me she'd put eyes on it. Have you seen any eyes? Look Oren, you know I'm not stupid. I'm not paranoid and I don't get my feelings hurt easy and I'm telling you that I am being watched. I am under the scope. Things are moving around me and I'm being kept out of the loop and that makes me really fucking nervous."

"What are you going to do?" Oren asked. "What should we do?"

"Hell if I know. One thing you have to do is keep an eye on Dani."

"An eye for what? All she does is run and clean."

"And invite strangers to stay with her." When Oren swore, Caldwell nodded. "Yeah, regardless of which side she's on, it can't be coincidence that she's got all these new friends out of the blue. Maybe the Charbaneaux kid is her connection to the agency. His family has a lot of connections way above my pay grade. On the other hand, he's known as the family fuck-up so maybe he's using Dani to take a walk on the dark side. And no matter how you slice it, her tie to Bermingham is no accident. Ain't nobody going to believe that."

"So what's her plan? How is this going to affect me?"

"Whatever she's going to do, she's going to deflect. If she's Bureau or she's dirty, she doesn't want you looking at her or either of her boys. If she's smart, she's going to create a distraction, some kind of snipe hunt to keep you looking one way while she or whoever she works for gets their job done."

CHAPTER FIFTEEN

2:30pm, 106° F

Tom had the decency to stay quiet as she led him to his room. In all of her nightmares, in all of her worst moments of terror, Dani had never imagined a scenario so surreal.

She was alone with Tom Booker once more.

And damn it if he didn't seem nervous again.

So now she walked along the gravel path, hearing his light steps behind her. The sun pounded down like a hammer. The heat from the planked path made the air shimmer, and bugs droned in the bougainvillea.

She wondered if she would die under one of these bushes.

Whoever had checked him in had put him in Room One at the end of the unit. Past Bermingham's room, separated from her shack by nothing more than a thick clump of sea grape.

Of course.

He didn't talk. He didn't stand too close. But she could feel his gaze on her as clearly as if he held her by the shoulders. He stayed back while she unlocked his door and Dani lost her nerve. She could not bring herself to step inside, to flip on the lights, and point out the refrigerator and show him how to keep the shower from leaking. No matter how disciplined her thoughts, her lifelong habit of being of two minds at once wasn't enough to let her close herself into a room with Tom Booker.

Maybe he sensed it because he gave her room to step away from the door before he went in. He hesitated in the doorway, looking into the dark space, the icy blast of air conditioning filtering out around him.

Dani watched the set of his shoulders, long muscles clear under his still-crisp white shirt. How did he manage that? Was it her imagination? He hadn't looked cold in the icy rain in DC; he didn't look hot or wilted in the humidity of Florida. She could almost convince herself that she was imagining him, that he was a ghost or a vision, if it hadn't been for that whole trying-to-kill-her thing.

"Did they send you?" She didn't know if she said it aloud.

Tom sighed, not turning around. "No. They don't know I'm here."

She believed him. One thing about Tom she knew, he didn't lie to her. She was grateful he didn't turn around. It felt easier to talk to him with his face out of sight.

"Why are you here?"

"To see you."

"Why?"

His shoulders shifted, dropping a little as if exhausted. "Don't you know?"

"No."

"Oh." He turned then just a little, just enough to see the fringe of his lashes, the slight downturn of his lower lip. She didn't know that expression and he didn't give her long to study it. "Oh," he said again and stepped inside. When he turned back to face her, the sunlight landed squarely across his face, his eyes brilliant against the shadows. "Then thank you, Dani. I guess I'll see you later."

"Sure." Later. Maybe when the Wheelers moored their boat and transferred the dangerous cargo to Bermingham, and who knew what other mayhem would ensue. Why not throw Tom Booker into the mix? "See you later."

He closed the door and she stood alone in the heat, wanting to run.

Instead she walked quietly, carefully, down the planked path. She walked past Bermingham's room, stepping into the wet sand and gravel of the lot to keep her passage quiet. Bermingham waited for her, she knew. He expected her to wait with him for the deal to go down. How exactly he wanted to pass the time she didn't know. She thought he'd wanted to sleep with her but now it felt more like he just wanted to collar her. Like a selfish child with too many toys, he didn't want to share her with anyone, even if he didn't want to play with her.

Mental box open. Mental box close. This was not the time to dwell on that.

She crossed the short end of the inlet, rounded the corner and passed the shuttered windows of the bait shop. Reggae still drifted softly from above, a few voices could be heard from the bar. Peg had that under control. For Peg it was just another day at Jinky's. Choo-Choo was off making a new life for himself on Casper's boat. And once again Dani was on the run. Dani had no safe place to hide, no asylum, nobody bigger than the monsters under her bed.

But maybe she did.

She walked the path to the water's edge where it disappeared behind a hedge of sea grape that matched the one by her shack. She stepped without looking over the debris hidden there to get to the path to Mr. Randolph's house. He didn't know what the story was with Bermingham. He thought she'd lied to him, but Mr. Randolph would listen to her. Mr. Randolph had given her a job and a place to stay. He'd given her a place to belong. He knew about dangerous people and helpless situations, didn't he? He would believe her. He might not know the same fears she did, but he knew fear.

She climbed onto the porch, making a point of crunching the gravel and stepping solidly on the steps. Mr. Randolph was nervous. She knew this deal had put him on edge and she didn't want to give any impression of sneaking up on him. This wasn't the time for stealth. She called his name before opening the screen door. Guitar music played more loudly than she'd ever heard him play. Maybe he used music to get him through tense scenes like this.

"Mr. Randolph? Boss? It's me, Dani."

She heard footsteps, glasses clinking, and for a moment she feared he had company. She didn't know what Mr. Randolph did in his private time. He never seemed to take any private time away from the bar. She waited outside the door, not looking in, and in a moment he appeared at the inside glass door. He opened it only a crack.

"What's up, Dani?"

She clasped her hands, nervous at the distance he kept from her. How could she convince him she wasn't the dragon to be kept at bay?

"Can I talk to you for a second?"

"Look, I acted like a jerk about Bermingham. You're young; he's good-looking. It's none of my business what you do when you're not working."

"It's not that."

"Is it your buddy, blondie? I already told you, he can stay with you. Again, it's none of my business. Casper said he'd give him a job, and if you two can fit into the shack, then be my—"

"It's not that either. Mr. Randolph, can I come in?"

His hesitation made the words that followed it unnecessary. "It's not really a good time."

From where she stood she knew she could reach the carport in twenty seconds at a dead run. She could be in the car, get the keys from the rip beneath the passenger's seat, and be halfway to Miami within the hour. She had thirty thousand dollars hidden inside the door panels; she could sacrifice what she'd left hidden in her shack.

She had two driver's licenses she'd swiped from the lost and found at Jinky's. But she had someone she trusted less than two feet from her and she couldn't make him listen.

"I'm in trouble."

Mr. Randolph snorted an unamused laugh. "Aren't we all? This is the day for it."

"No, it's something else. It's someone else. There's a man. Here. He found me."

"A man? Here? You know, Dani, most people can't find this place with a map and a GPS. Suddenly we have a lot of traffic. Why do you suppose that is?"

Dani didn't think she could answer him but the price of silence was too high. "Mr. Randolph, I know this looks really weird. I know you're worried about the deal going down with the Wheelers; I am too. But this guy, this guy you rented a room to for the month? He's like nothing you've ever seen. I know Bermingham has this reputation, but Tom Booker? I know what Tom Booker can do. I'm one of the people he tried to do it to."

Mr. Randolph looked down, rubbing the back of his neck, and Dani could see the signs of her boss reconsidering. She didn't dare breathe.

"Is he the one who shot you?"

She wanted to lie. She'd never be able to explain about the CIA sniper and her old boss and Booker with his horrible knives. But if she lied now, if he saw her lie—

"No." He sighed and looked past her again and Dani rushed to explain. "But he was there. He was part of it. It's hard. I can't really . . . there isn't any way I can tell you."

"So you can't tell me, but you want me to help you. Help you do what, Dani? Keep an eye on him? Maybe tell my buddy Caldwell about him? I mean, you do know what Caldwell does for a living, right? You know who he works for, what he does. You're a smart girl. You pay attention, don't you?"

It was so similar to what Bermingham had said to her just hours ago that Dani's overworked internal alarm system set off yet another flash of caution. "It doesn't seem like that's much of a secret. Is it supposed to be? Do you think he could help me?"

XXX

There it was. Oren had never thought himself any kind of genius but he'd always considered himself a pretty decent judge of character. He'd had the lazy addict's keen sense of who would fuck with him the least and he thought he'd never lost it. Shysters and conmen and users and chiselers, he'd seen them come and go and lost very little to any of them. And he'd prided himself on handling almost all of them with a friendly, sun-and-vodka-soaked charm.

But now this dark little girl with those serious brown eyes, who had crawled up into his life like some wounded wild animal that would suddenly permit him to feed her by hand, was turning out to be every inch the predator Caldwell painted her to be.

Here was the misdirect. This Tom Booker, this dangerous man who just happened to show up on Redemption on the weekend Bermingham made his play for control. She wanted his help; she wanted Caldwell's help, even though just a day before she wouldn't have spit on the agent if he were on fire. She wanted both men to be looking at this new stranger, protecting the tiny damsel in distress, so she and the people she worked for could tee them both up to be in the absolute wrong place at the wrong time. That place could be at ground zero of a federal bust or it could be at the messy end of Bermingham's cleanup. Either way, that place would suck and Oren didn't want to be there. He didn't want to find out that his buddy Caldwell's worst-case scenario could be far worse than either man imagined.

Shit, he really didn't want Caldwell to be right at all.

He wanted to punch Dani and punch himself and keep punching until somebody made this situation right, but Oren hadn't survived Jinky and his own wasted youth by ignoring very clear signs of obvious danger. He knew he could trust Caldwell; that was one thing he didn't question. So Oren bit back his anger and his almost overwhelming urge to beg Dani to explain herself to him. If she was a liar, she was an excellent one and there was too much at stake to risk falling under her spell.

"I don't know what you want me to do, Dani. I'm your boss, not your dad." The words tasted sour on his tongue so he spit them out as quickly as possible. "And I don't need to borrow any trouble, especially not now. You want to call the law on that guy, be my guest. But don't bring that shit into Jinky's, you hear me?"

X X X

She stood there as he slid the glass door shut, turned his back on her, and headed deeper into his house. She wanted to say that he was the one who rented the room to Tom Booker; he was the one who brought the killer to Redemption Key.

But she didn't say that because she knew that was a lie.

CHAPTER SIXTEEN

She didn't know how long she stood there. The sun beat down like it was trying to set the world on fire. It was a perfect day for it. This was a day when everything should burn. And the world didn't even know it was coming to an end.

Dani thought about how nice it would be to drive. She could drive north, over the hundred little channels, over the staggering expanse of Seven Mile Bridge, being blinded by the glare off the water until she hit the mainland. She could keep driving. She could ignore the ache she knew she'd feel in her shoulder from sitting so long, the throb of the gunshot wound in her leg, until she fell out of the car wherever she ran out of gas. More gas, more driving, chewing espresso beans to keep her awake until she cleared Florida, maybe Louisiana, maybe Arkansas.

She could trade in her car, sacrifice her beloved little Honda for a head start evading the federal fuckers who would no doubt start looking for her. It would be a hard price to pay but it would be worth it to send those blunt-headed sons of bitches on a wild goose chase through the bayou or through Texas or Kansas. Let them think she'd gone back to Oklahoma.

Like Choo-Choo had.

Dani walked the planked path without looking. Of course they'd find her. Everyone who wanted to find her would and the one person she wanted to stay with would lose her again. Would Choo-Choo care? Would he understand or figure she had her reasons? Would he take her place at Jinky's or settle in with Casper's crew and figure she was just another shit friend using him when she felt like she needed him?

Could she wait for him to come back from Casper's boat? Take him with her? Would he go? He came to Florida. Dani tripped on a loose board at the broken corner of the old dock behind the hedge, turning her ankle against a rusted boat cleat. She felt the waxy sea grape stick to her skin as she bent to see blood drip down her foot. Who was she kidding? It didn't matter if Choo-Choo was with her or not. It didn't matter if Bermingham tied her up in the hull of his boat to a shipment of nuclear warheads bound for Syria or if Caldwell brought a battalion of Feds in to throw a net over her.

Tom Booker had found her.

Mr. Randolph couldn't understand it. The Wheelers and Bermingham and all the badge-waving assholes who had and would surround her were nothing in the face of those wide blue eyes, that unblinking gaze that took Dani in like he owned her. No, like he'd made her, built her from scratch, like he knew her from the inside out. Even Choo-Choo wouldn't understand. Her friend had seen Tom, had heard snippets of the long conversations he and Dani had shared on that endless night in DC, but Tom had been focused only on her. Choo-Choo hadn't been pinned to the wall by those strong, steady hands. He hadn't seen the force with which Tom had come at her with not one but two blades.

He had asked her, "Are you going to kill me, Dani?"

She'd told him yes. She had wanted to kill him and she'd relived that question over and over in a hundred nightmares. She'd thrown herself over a railing that night, willing to take her own life if it meant strangling Tom Booker, and what had she gotten for it? Scars and nightmares and a permanent federal tail. That psychotic son of a bitch didn't even get a scratch. And he certainly didn't get jail time.

She stood on the little abandoned dock, looking out toward the spot on the channel bridge that she jumped from every day. She wouldn't leave Choo-Choo alone to face whatever was coming down at Jinky's. Bermingham and Mr. Randolph and Special fucking Agent Daniel Caldwell thought they had Dani all figured out, that they knew her place and had some right to put her there. But what had Choo-Choo said last night at the airport? He did nothing but want and hate.

Choo-Choo was the only person who felt exactly the way she did.

She didn't know who she'd run into first—Bermingham or Booker—so she kept her head down as she headed back to Jinky's. She circled around the front, wanting to stay out of sight from anyone on the inlet as long as possible. The tinny sound of a bike bell made her jump. Throwing gravel to either side, a long-legged figure turned off the road, steering toward her. She saw long, brown shorts, a wide-brimmed straw hat, orange-rimmed sunglasses perched on a nose covered in zinc oxide, all of it eclipsed by the glare of a T-shirt in a shade of neon green found only on highway crews.

She stared as Choo-Choo skidded to a halt, pulling the plastic sunglasses off to hang from their equally tacky neon orange string. He grinned at her.

"I've decided to blend."

Dani squinted against the glare of his shirt. "With who? Wham?"

He laughed. "Obscure, but I like it. I got the job. Casper hired me as first mate for his sunset cruise tonight. I suspect this will involve swabbing a good deal of tourist vomit."

"So he stripped you of all your clothes and dressed you like that?"

"This?" Choo-Choo looked down at his shirt. "No, this was from a man renting one of Casper's rowboats. It's from someplace called"—he pulled the front of the shirt out to read the writing on the breast—"the Lizard's Thicket in Gatlinburg, Tennessee. This guy admired my Black Dog shirt, said he'd always wanted to go to Cape Cod; I said this would get him closer, and we swapped shirts. Now I smell like fish heads and," he sniffed the collar, "corn dogs, I think."

Dani shook her head. "I'm trying to figure out who got the better end of this deal. If there even was a better end." Choo-Choo laughed again.

"You're right about this place, Dani. I don't know if it's the heat—and God, this heat—or the silence or the tiny little deer that are everywhere, but I love it." He leaned forward on the handlebars. Sweat-glued blond strands against his face beneath the hat. "I feel like there's this thing, this stone, that's moving inside my chest. I always hated sailing. Hated it. Then when I climbed on that rust bucket tub of Casper's and smelled all that sunscreen and recycled margaritas, I just thought, 'I can do this.' I'm going to do this."

He rocked forward on the bike, nudging her with the wheel. The brim of his hat flopped down as he cocked his head to look at her. "What's that face? I thought you'd be glad I'm adjusting. Are you worried I'm going to lose my keen fashion sense? Because I assure you, I can rock this T-shirt."

She wanted to laugh, to assure him she didn't doubt his fashion sensibilities. She wanted to tell him she was glad he liked it here, but she couldn't because she wasn't. If he'd been miserable here, it would be so much easier to tell him.

"Tom found me. He's here."

She watched the news sink in. Choo-Choo's smile dimmed, then dropped, as did his foot from the pedal, making him stagger in place. He stared at her, open-mouthed.

"Where? How did he . . ."

Dani shrugged, not wanting to talk. She knew once she said it out loud, it would be real. "He's in Room One. The one at the end, just on the other side of the bushes from my shack. He's there right now. I let him in."

He stared past her, toward the units, as if expecting to see Tom Booker materialize on demand. "Are you going to do something?"

"Like?"

"Call the police? The state police? Hell, the FBI. Why don't you tell your boss to tell his Fibbie buddy about him? Tom's here." He gave up trying to balance on the bike and stood straddling the bar. "He killed all those people. The FBI has to know, right?"

She nodded, watching the understanding dawn on his face as she spoke. "Yeah, they must know. How could they not? I mean, he's here. He's out. He looks great. Not a single fucking scar on him. They patched him up nice and carefully, Choo-Choo. Not like us."

"Not like us." He sat back heavily on the bike seat, his hands dropping to his sides. The handlebars spun, the wheel slapping Dani in the leg, but they both ignored it. "They let him out."

"I don't think they just let him out. I think they turned him out." Saying the words aloud fueled something hot inside her. "They fixed him up, made sure he was just fine, and they put him to work. Again. All that shit he told me on the phone about not knowing who hired him that night—maybe he didn't know then, but he sure as hell knows now."

"What are you going to do?"

"I'm going to run." It felt right as she said it. "I've got almost forty thousand dollars stashed around here, most of it in my car. There's a tracking device in my car so we'll have to ditch it once we get to the mainland but—"

"We?"

She gripped the handlebar before her. All those months ago, that lifetime ago when she'd been running for her life in DC, Choo-Choo could have left her but he didn't. She'd repaid him by leaving him in that hospital. "He wouldn't know you by sight." She tried to laugh. "Especially in that outfit. You could stay. You could just leave on your own."

Choo-Choo pulled his cell phone from his pocket. "Because it's worked out so well for me on my own these past few months. Fuck it." He whipped his arm over his head, sending the phone sailing into the water behind Dani. "Fuck this place. Fuck Tom Booker. And fuck that fucking tracking device. Let's steal a boat."

"What?" Dani felt such a rush of relief that he'd go with her she could hardly follow what he said. "What boat?"

"Let's steal that one." He pointed over her shoulder, out to the open water of the channel. "We'll take a kayak out, climb on board, and steal the son of a bitch before anyone is the wiser."

Dani squinted out over the water into the glare of the lowering afternoon sun. She knew nothing about boats but she could tell this was little more than a tub. It rose and fell in the gentle tide, shifting until she could read the peeling paint.

"We can't steal that boat. That's the *Pied Piper*. That's the Wheelers' boat."

X X X

2:43pm, 106° F

Caldwell poured his friend another drink, which Oren ignored. Vodka wouldn't cut the bitter taste in his mouth. He didn't know which would be worse—finding out for sure that Dani was playing him or finding out that he'd shut her out when she was really in trouble. He knew one thing for sure. For the first time in more than a decade, Oren Randolph yearned for something harder than vodka.

"I'm going to get out of here," Caldwell said softly. Oren figured he wore his misery all over his face and the agent must be able to see it. "Let me head back to Miami, see what I can find out. Maybe I'm a paranoid old man who's manufacturing drama where there is none. Maybe my SSA has a team coming down to bust the Wheelers as we speak. Hell, they may be doing me a solid and protecting you as my CI."

"Yeah," Oren said, giving in and grabbing the vodka, "because I know how high a priority they place on burned-out ex-cokehead bar owners. Shit, Caldwell, what if Dani was telling the truth? What if she's in trouble?"

Caldwell clapped his hand on Oren's shoulder. "Man, we are all in trouble. When the Wheelers are moving something this big and we've got a gun like Bermingham on site, we are all in trouble. My advice to you is to lay low. Keep your door closed. Let them do whatever the hell they're going to do out there. If Dani is telling the truth, if there really is some psycho out there looking for her, odds are he's going to get caught in the crossfire. Sometimes you get lucky and situations like this take care of themselves."

"I don't feel very lucky."

"Then let's make our own luck. Let's up our odds and get out of here. Just for the night. I'm parked across the road on the other side of the hedge. Nobody saw me come in, nobody will see me go out. Give me five minutes, then you go around front. If they ask, tell them you're taking your evening constitutional. Tell them they have the run of the place until you get back. Tell them you've got a date. Tell them anything, just get the hell out of there."

"Bermingham's not going to let that happen. He's jumpy. He's watching. And—oh no, is that a boat?" Oren cocked his head, years of experience letting him pick up the sound of a small motorboat approaching the dock.

"Bermingham isn't going anywhere. You said he told you the deal can't go down until dawn. He's probably going to be spinning Dani around on his lap like a top—"

"Aw man, don't say tha—"

Caldwell gripped Oren's arm tight. "You don't owe that little girl anything. Like you told her, she's an employee, not your daughter. You gave her a job and a place to live; she does what you tell her. If she's fucking you, leave her ass hanging. If she's not, she's a smart girl. Something tells me she knows how to get out of the way." He loosened his grip and patted Oren's arm. "And surely by now she knows how to collect fifteen bucks for the public dock, okay? I'm going. Five minutes, then you make your excuses. Then we get our asses up to Miami until the dust settles."

Oren nodded, hating every inch of the plan and not just because he hated Miami. Caldwell downed the last of his drink and moved to the sliding glass door. He peered through the glass before sliding the door open slowly. He had one foot out the door when he turned back to Oren to give him an encouraging nod. He got half a nod out before the muzzle of a gun pressed against his temple.

CHAPTER SEVENTEEN

2:59pm, 106° F

They heard Bermingham swearing before they saw him clear the hedge of bougainvillea at the corner of the walkway. Dani put her hand on Choo-Choo's arm to still him as the Canadian charged past them without looking. He was shouting into his phone and then shouting at Juan Wheeler, who pulled up to the outside slip in a dinghy.

"The fuck is this, Wheeler? You're early." Bermingham didn't wait for Juan to tie off the boat. He leaned down, shouting at the smaller man, who ignored him. "Vincente hasn't said anything about moving this up. Is my cargo on board? Get Vincente on the phone now."

Choo-Choo laid his bike down silently in the gravel and he and Dani crept toward the units, putting distance between themselves and the scene at the dock. Dani could tell by the light it had to be close to three o'clock. The sun wouldn't be setting for a while. That meant hours of hot, direct sunlight on whatever the Wheelers were selling to Bermingham. She didn't have to hear all the words to pick up Bermingham's opinion of the situation.

Choo-Choo whispered in her ear. "This might be an ideal time to put that 'running for our lives' plan into motion."

XXX

2:30pm, 106° F

The first thing Booker did after Dani left was turn off the air-conditioning. The heat didn't bother him but the inability to hear sounds outside his room did. He slid the old metal window open and surveyed the empty dock slips. He'd seen Dani follow the planked walkway back toward the main building and around the thick greenery that hung over the water. Was that where Dani lived? The thought of slipping into her private living space again sent a shimmer of anticipation along his skin.

First things first, however. Booker changed into something a little less conspicuous—the khaki shorts and a faded T-shirt he'd bought in Atlanta. The clothes made him feel silly. He liked long pants and button-down shirts. Anywhere else they helped him remain invisible, but blending in at a fishing camp in Florida required him to stretch his comfort zone a little. It would be worth it if it made Dani feel more at ease around him. He drew the line at sandals, however. He felt off balance enough as it was. He hadn't gone without socks in over thirty years; he wasn't going to start now. Again, while he preferred hard black shoes, canvas sneakers and white socks would have to do.

He didn't look at himself in the mirror as he stepped into the bathroom. Memories of being a young boy in sneakers and a ball cap tried to distract him but Booker had more than enough experience to hold them back. It didn't matter that this wasn't technically a job. It was a mission, however undefined, and he had procedures to follow. Clipping the sheath of his new serrated knife onto the waistband of his shorts helped him relax so he went ahead and strapped his smaller blade to his right ankle, pulling his sock up to hide it. He probably wouldn't need them but their presence helped soothe his nerves.

With a little effort, he finished the last step of his settling-in process. The screen in the small window over the toilet resisted him but a two-handed punch finally knocked it free of the frame. He'd pay the damage deposit if necessary. Stepping lightly onto the toilet seat, Booker slid through the small window, lowering himself to the gravel below. He always felt better with an exit plan.

He stayed close to the laundry bins and recycling dumpsters behind the units, moving into the shadows of the low palm trees that ringed the gravel lot, not to avoid the sun but to keep from casting too long a shadow of his own. He could hear voices across the narrow inlet and the faint chug of a motor out on the water but nothing really shattered the heat silence of Jinky's. Still, Booker felt better in the shadows.

His breath caught when he saw Dani in that little dress leaning over the handlebars of some man's bike. The guy was lanky, his face hidden under a straw hat, but something in his build triggered recognition. It wasn't the big guy from the bar, but he'd seen him somewhere before. Booker made himself comfortable between a thick clump of bougainvillea and the sign listing the docking rules. With the sun heading toward the horizon over the open water, he knew the shadows would shift and lengthen, keeping him hidden for a while. He hoped Dani would stay right where she was.

Of course someone had to ruin it. Someone big. Booker stayed still as a tall man in a golf shirt stormed past him, swearing into a cell phone. That was the guy from the bar. He watched Dani's reaction, seeing how she stilled herself and her companion, like a deer caught in the open. Booker couldn't imagine how anyone wouldn't notice her tan arms and black hair, how her skin shone in the sun, but the guy on the phone only had eyes for the dinghy motoring up to the last docking slip.

Booker had no interest in the shouting man or the greasy little fellow tying his boat up but he was fascinated by Dani's reaction. She and her friend all but slithered toward him, their eyes glued on the fight breaking out on the dock in front of Jinky's. Booker didn't doubt there would be gunplay; tempers like that in this kind of heat usually led to explosive violence. What he wondered was how much Dani knew about the exchange.

She had certainly proven her knack for being in the thick of trouble.

Dani and her friend passed less than two yards in front of him, their backs to him while they watched the fight escalating on the dock. He almost risked ducking back into the thorny shrub but knew if he made any noise at all she might turn. How would he explain that? He felt stupid enough as it was wearing shorts in the first place. So he stayed still, watching her watch the men. He watched a rivulet of sweat slide down between her shoulder blades.

"Shit." The word was a breath from her lips.

The men on the dock weren't alone any longer. Two more men stepped out from behind the bushes that hung over the walkway at the edge of the water, the same walkway Dani had taken when she'd left him earlier. The two men, one in his late fifties, the other not much younger, didn't look very happy to be taking their walk and it only took a second for Booker to see why. Behind them, holding a gun, walked a lumpy, leering man who, if possible, seemed even greasier than the little fellow who'd climbed from the motorboat.

"Huh," Booker said under his breath. This looked interesting.

XXX

2:59pm, 107° F

Any doubts Oren might have had about the seriousness of the situation evaporated the instant he saw Joaquin Wheeler pressing the semi-automatic to Caldwell's temple. The look in the greasy man's good eye told him that Oren's protected status with the Wheelers had officially come to an end. Joaquin didn't have to speak. Oren rose and joined Caldwell at the door, letting himself be pushed toward Jinky's. It was then he saw the *Pied Piper* anchored fifty or so yards out in the channel. That made it almost ten hours early.

One look at Bermingham's red face told Oren how well the Canadian had taken the change in schedule. Juan leaned against the dock post smirking as Bermingham yelled at him and at whoever he had on the phone. The Wheelers might have been intimidated by Bermingham when the deal began, but something had changed. Vincente must have decided to throw his weight around, reassert his dominance. Oren heard Caldwell sigh.

This was going to end badly.

"You listen to me, you slimy little fuck." Bermingham pressed the phone to his ear, bending a bit as if his height could intimidate just by voice alone. "We had a deal. You know what happens to this merchandise in the heat. You think you can fuck with me? You think I'm just going to sit here and watch that ship bake? I'm boarding. I'm boarding and I'm taking the shipment. Your money will be there."

Oren couldn't hear the other side of the conversation—Vincente, he assumed. The Canadian shut his eyes to what he heard, pressing the heel of his palm against his forehead as if holding back a massive headache. When he opened them once more and saw Oren and Caldwell at the end of Joaquin's gun, he scowled.

"One hour," he said into the phone, his glare moving over the crowd on the dock. "You have one hour to get this straight, you hear me, you little . . . Shit." Bermingham stared at the phone and then shoved it in his pocket. "What the fuck is this?"

"This," Juan said, waving his hands over his brother and his brother's hostages, "is the reason we showed up ahead of schedule. You think you can screw with Mr. Vincente? Huh? You think this is the first time some two-bit player like you has tried to run us?"

Bermingham shook his head. "The fuck are you talking about?

These guys are nothing. Randolph here was the set-up; I don't know who the hell this other joker is. His boyfriend?"

"Let me tell you who this is." Juan curled his lip. "That right there is Special Agent Daniel Caldwell of the FBI. Save your fake surprise. Mr. Vincente said you'd try something. Mr. Vincente thinks you're a rat and when Mr. Vincente smells a rat, you know what he does?"

Oren could tell Juan wanted to insert a pause for dramatic effect. He'd seen the tweaker try it before. He failed as always, stumbling over his own words with spastic chatter.

"He shoots them. He shoots the rats. Mr. Vincente shoots rats."

Only Joaquin appreciated his brother's delivery, wheezing out a giggle of approval. Oren felt an odd sense of resignation settle over him. He knew the Wheelers; he'd been unlucky enough to be present for enough confrontations to know how this played out. Someone was going to get shot and very soon. He only hoped it was Bermingham.

Bermingham looked from Juan to Joaquin and back again, his scowl changing into a look of disbelief. "You think I brought in a Fed? You think I hauled my ass all the way down here from Montreal to bring in a Fed to break up the deal I've spent a month setting up?" He smiled at Oren as if the two of them were old buddies. "Can you believe this guy, Randolph? I mean, I'm the outsider here. I'm the one with my ass on the line if this deal gets busted and this beaner thinks I'm bringing in the Feds. Hey Randolph?"

Oren really wished the Canadian would leave him out of this.

"Randolph, what do you think Vincente would say—"

"That's Mister Vincente," Joaquin said with enough spit to make Caldwell flinch.

"What do you think Vincente would say," Bermingham continued, eyes on Oren, "if he found out that the man he brokered the deal with, the man he sent his two idiot puppets to, was keeping a Fed tucked away in his back pocket? Huh? Who do you think this is going to blow back on? Me? I don't think so. Hey, maybe not even you, Randolph. No, I think if this blows back on anyone, it's going to be on the guys who are running the deal, the flunkies, the lackies, the red shirts. You know what I mean?"

Oren didn't bother to answer.

Bermingham looked at each Wheeler and laughed. "I'm talking about you morons. Juan, you. And your brother or whoever the fuck that fat walleyed bastard is with the gun. This is your turf, Juan. If anyone brought a Fed in, it was you."

He waited for Juan to absorb the meaning of his words. Wisely, Oren thought, he didn't check to see when Joaquin would catch on. It was hot out here and clearly Bermingham didn't have all day. Once Juan caught up, he pulled a gun from his pocket and raised it to Bermingham.

"I didn't bring any fucking Fed in. Mr. Vincente knows I'm loyal. Mr. Vincente said that we were supposed to check for any dirt. Mr. Vincente said that if we saw even a hint of anything shady we're supposed to blow the boat."

"Bullshit."

"Bullshit, bullshit," Juan said, fishing in his other pocket for a key fob. "See this? It's wired to the engine. One push of this button and the whole boat goes boom." He was bright enough to read Bermingham's smirk. "And before you get any fancy ideas, know this. If I don't call Mr. Vincente from the cell phone on the boat within two hours, he can detonate the bomb remotely. He had us rig up that boat real nice, just to be sure everyone holds up their end."

Juan swung his gun wildly when he heard the heavy footsteps of Bermingham's buddy Ned heading their way. It seemed the sight of the Wheelers with guns still didn't unnerve the quiet, muscular man. He sauntered up to his partner, looked around the scene, and raised a questioning eyebrow.

Bermingham shook his head. "Seems Vincente wants to get ahead of schedule."

"We moving the cargo early? Good. Get out of this freaking heat."

"You're not moving anything!" Juan waved his gun around, trying and failing to get Ned to notice it. "You and your buddy here are going to wait until Mr. Vincente gets his money. Anyone makes a move to get in that boat, I blow it sky high." He jumped at the sound of another motorboat. "Who the fuck is this?"

XXX

_3:03pm, 106° F_

Booker shifted against the post. The acoustics in this inlet were terrific. It helped that the little greasy one with the high-pitched voice was facing the section of Jinky's under the porch. His voice echoed back across the water. The big one and his muscular friend both spoke with deeper tones that carried nicely across the water. He could make out almost every word they were saying. He looked forward to seeing who would kill whom first.

What did they call this? A busman's holiday?

Or would he have to do some killing to make that true?

Either way, Booker felt content to watch the action play out with no involvement from him. He did wonder what, if anything, Dani had to do with this. She seemed to have known very well to get clear of the action. He squinted to see the misshapen man holding the older men at gunpoint and grimaced. He hoped Dani never had to have any interactions with him. He looked unsavory to say the least.

He was relieved of the need to dwell on the thought by the arrival of another motorboat.

XXX

_3:03pm, 106° F_

Dani peered out from behind the thick hedge of sea grape to watch the fight escalating in front of Jinky's. She and Choo-Choo had slipped behind the rental units and made it all the way to Dani's shack at the edge of the water. The plan had been to sneak back to grab a few necessities and the rest of her cash and haul ass out of Jinky's parking lot as soon as possible. Where they hid, the wind off the water made hearing Bermingham's conversation impossible, but they could both make out the angry tones and read the body language. The guns helped drive the point home.

"They're not going to let us just drive out of here." Choo-Choo leaned his head back against the shack wall.

"Maybe we could steal the boat, after all," Dani said. "Both the Wheelers are on shore. If we could get to the boat without them seeing us, we could climb up. Do you know how to hotwire a boat? Is that possible?"

"How would we get out there unseen? The boat seems to be the focus of attention. They'd see us in a kayak or a rowboat."

"We could swim. I swim farther than that every day."

Choo-Choo made a soft sound and Dani turned to see him staring at her. He pulled the collar of his T-shirt down to expose the edge of his scars. "Let's just say the days of holding my breath are behind me. I can barely light a cigarette. Maybe we could just lay low?"

"That's probably a good idea." She heard the putter of a small motor. "Who's this?" Peering through the sea grape again, she swore under her breath. "You've got to be kidding me."

X X X

3:03pm, 106° F

"You've got to be kidding me," Oren muttered when he saw the little boat overloaded with Australians puttering up to the dock. Dreadlocks and beach towels hung over the edge as the suntanned group laughed and sang, oblivious to the scene awaiting them. They pulled into the slip beside Juan, throwing the lines out toward the cleats, followed by two coolers that clinked with empty bottles.

Ned stepped closer to their boat, putting a heavy foot down on the line. Nigel/Rigel tossed a heap of wet towels over his foot, squinting up at the big man. "Tie us off there, would ya? That's a good man."

"You should go," Ned said.

"We just got back, yeah. Good day out there. Got some pics of your little deer and some amazing shots of heron." He helped two of his buddies up onto the dock while the one Oren was mostly sure was a woman tied off the boat. "Now we're ready for some nice frosty ones, right?"

Oren didn't think he had ever seen any group of living creatures so oblivious.

All but the girl fished phones from their pockets, laughing as they showed each other photos. Ned gave Bermingham a questioning glance, stepping aside as the taller man approached Nigel/Rigel.

"You should go," Bermingham said, physically blocking the dreadlocked boy from moving past him. Finally the kid thought to look up.

"Yeah, yeah, we're going. Heading up to get us some of your shit beer. Gotta do what you gotta do, you know?"

Bermingham didn't move. "The bar is closed."

The kids laughed. "Nah," the maybe-girl said. "We're staying here. We're regulars."

"Is that right?" Bermingham smiled and stepped closer to the three holding their cell phones in front of them. Faster than they could react—which Oren had to admit probably wasn't all that fast— he snatched all three phones, one after another, and tossed them into the water. At their cries of outrage, he drew his weapon from his shorts pocket, pressing it between the eyes of the closest boy.

177

"Maybe you didn't understand what I said. Maybe it's the accent. I said the bar is closed. Which room are you staying in?" When nobody spoke he pressed hard, making the boy's eyes water. "If you can't say the number, stomp it out with your feet. What room?"

"Six! Six!" Nigel/Rigel sputtered.

"Good boy." Bermingham smiled. "Now unless you want me to start shooting into the empty space my gun's pointing at, you're all going to go back to your room, shut the door, and keep your fucking mouths shut. Ned, get that kid's phone. Toss it in the water."

Nigel/Rigel didn't resist and Bermingham nodded. "Very good. Are we clear now? You go into your room and you stay there. If I see you, I shoot you. If I see cops, I shoot them and then I shoot you. If I see anyone at all walking around out here, I shoot everyone, but it always comes back to me shooting you too. Understand? Get out of here."

Nigel/Rigel finally found a shred of nerve. "Welcome to fucking America."

Ned laughed. "We're Canadian."

CHAPTER EIGHTEEN

They watched the Australians hurry back to their room. Choo-Choo whispered into Dani's ear. "They're not worried about witnesses. Why do you suppose that is?"

"Is it just me? Us? Does shit like this happen to everyone?" She stepped backwards, pushing him with her out of the shrubbery and back around her shed. It took all of her self-control not to kick over the stand of paddles leaning against the wall. "They're not going to let anyone walk away from this. Even if Bermingham leaves with his cargo, the Wheelers are going to blow those kids away. They're not going to leave them to be witnesses. Maybe they'll let Mr. Randolph go. Maybe. And only then because they'll be able to use him again." She stopped her rant. "What?"

Choo-Choo shrugged. "Maybe that's not the only reason they'll let your boss live. Maybe he's not just your boss."

"Don't go there. Mr. Randolph is scared of these guys."

"But still does business with them."

"He doesn't have a choice."

179

"Oh." His tone told her just how much he believed that. "Well, regardless of who is working for whom, nobody is working for us. What do you want to do? Think they'll just leave us alone? Let us ride this out? That Bermingham guy seems to favor you. And you've already told me about the delightful rapport you have with, what's his name? Joaquin?"

"Shh."

Heavy footsteps approached on the wooden walkway. "Dani?"

She didn't recognize the voice. Yanking Choo-Choo by the arm, she jerked him toward the laundry carts pushed up beside the paddle stand. "Tell them I'm not here." She ducked down between the bins, pulling her feet up close, and shooed him away. Fortunately nobody could assume a look of bored insouciance quicker or more effectively than Choo-Choo and when Bermingham's thug, Ned, looked around the corner to the back of the shed, Choo-Choo leaned against the paddle stand as if he'd been planted there. He didn't even bother to arch an eyebrow.

"Who are you?"

"I'm Sinclair. Hi there." He made his tone just lurid enough to make the larger man pause. "Something I can help you with?"

"Where's Dani?"

"Running. She's always running."

Not a second's hesitation. Dani smiled.

"Damn it," Ned muttered. "Tell her when she gets back to get her ass to the bar ASAP."

"Can do."

Ned still didn't walk away. "No, you're staying with her, right? You'd better come with me. Come on."

"To the bar? With you? Maybe you should tell me your name first, soldier."

"Save it for the health club, pal. C'mon."

Choo-Choo didn't move. From where she sat she could just make out his rear profile. From what she could see, if he got any more relaxed he'd collapse. "Quick question. If I'm with you, who's going to tell Dani to hurry back to Jinky's? She usually showers after her run, sometimes naps. She might miss all the fun. How about we do this? I stay here and wait for her and the instant her little feet hit this doorway, I'll hustle us both over to your party. It's not like I'm going to be able to sneak away, not in this shirt."

She could hear Ned scuffing the gravel. "Give me your phone."

"Don't have one."

"Bullshit. Everyone's got a phone."

"I don't. But if I did I'd give you my number." Choo-Choo took a step closer. "You're welcome to search me if it would make you feel better."

"Knock it off." Dani heard him mutter to himself for a moment. "Okay, look. Here's what we're going to do. You are going to sit in front of this, this—what is this? A cabin?"

Dani could hear the smirk in Choo-Choo's voice. "Home."

"Whatever. You sit there in front where I can see you. You keep that shirt on and stay out in the open until Dani gets back. Then you two double-time it to the bar. I'll tell you the same thing we told those morons on the boat: If I see you or I see any signs of anyone you called doing anything other than what I told you to do, I'll shoot you. And I promise you this, blondie. I will be the one that shoots you."

Choo-Choo sighed. "I've heard that before."

Footsteps away across the gravel and Dani risked leaning forward enough to see Choo-Choo's profile. His high cheekbones glowed with a blush that hadn't been there before. He didn't look down at her but stared out at the hedges and the water beyond. He stayed where Ned could see him but turned enough to hear Dani's whisper.

"You okay?"

His mouth worked in that tight way she'd come to recognize. She knew those high spots of color on his cheeks. Choo-Choo was pissed.

"If he had put a hand on me . . ."

"I think your come-hither act put the kibosh on that."

Choo-Choo snorted. "Don't kid yourself. That's exactly the kind of guy who'll come sneaking around the back door after a few too many brewskis with his buddies."

Dani stood and moved closer behind him. She kept her voice low and even, knowing she was stoking the fire that already burned within her. "Just another ham-fisted jack-off with a gun. Another bully who gets to pick and choose who lives and who dies."

"Another fucking authority. Another little despot." He stared straight ahead, his eyes shining with anger. "I don't want to get shot again, even if my scars get the bar their twenty-fourth round of fucking drinks. But if I do get shot, I'm not going to be the only one paying. I'm not. I'm not going back to that place."

She knew what he meant. She knew that place. It was the place of her nightmares.

"Then we need a plan."

"We need a gun." He chewed his lip. "No other way off this island?"

"That bridge is it. I can't see us kayaking our way out."

"Then we need a distraction."

They stood there silently, thinking, listening to the faint sound of angry voices drifting across the water. Dani smiled.

"How do you sink a boat?"

X X X

3:38pm, 106° F

She swam against the tide. That was good. She ran her instructions over and over in her mind. Choo-Choo had sat in the doorway of the shack, whispering to her before she snuck through the hedges to the water. He had told her that she wouldn't need to create any hole. If she managed to disconnect the bilge pump before she unscrewed the clamps on the hoses attached to the metal tubes in the through hull, the boat would sink quickly. Even with his detailed descriptions, she wasn't sure exactly what these metal tubes were, although the term 'through hull' seemed pretty self-explanatory. And she could certainly find a circuit breaker to pull the pump wires. She planned on unplugging and unscrewing anything she could get her hands on.

Once the boat started to sink, the plan was to swim back to the floating kayak dock. If Bermingham watched the boat, he'd see it start to go down and raise the alarm. All eyes would be on the boat and the tide would be in her favor. She could climb out of the water behind the heavy greenery on the far side of the inlet and hurry with Choo-Choo to her car. At least one or two of the men would jump in the dinghy and the sound of its motor would distract them from the sound of the Honda's engine.

It wasn't a great plan, but it was a damn sight better than sitting around waiting to die.

Plus Bermingham and the Wheelers would lose all their precious cargo.

Dani didn't know what the boat held. At first she'd thought drugs but judging from everyone's nervousness, she had to guess it was something more serious. Something that became delicate in the heat. It had to be weapons. Heat wouldn't bother guns but it would probably bother explosives, and twenty-five volatile units of deadly explosives didn't belong in the hands of Bermingham and definitely not in the hands of the Wheelers.

Whatever they were coddling in the hull of this tub was going to find a new home at the bottom of the Spanish Channel. Dani didn't bother telling herself she was doing this for the good of mankind. She wished she could see their faces when they watched the boat disappear.

She wished she could see their faces when they realized she too had disappeared.

But first things first. She swam in long, smooth strokes, staying underwater as long as possible to keep the chances of being spotted from shore to a minimum. The lowering sun would only help, shining brilliantly on the water, darkening shadows and throwing a powerful glare. A heavy-duty screwdriver hung from her neck on the orange string from Choo-Choo's sunglasses. That was all she'd need, he told her. Get below decks and start wreaking havoc.

If she could get on the boat.

She squinted through the water to be sure she didn't surface in the shadow of the boat. If anyone was watching, she'd be visible against the trawler's faded red hull. Instead she peeked out at the back of the boat—stern? Aft? She had no idea. There, as Choo-Choo had predicted, was a nice, shiny ladder nearly reaching the water. Choo-Choo had seen enough of Joaquin Wheeler to know the big man wouldn't be comfortable shimmying down a flimsy ladder to the dinghy. He'd told Dani the odds were excellent the boys would have brought along a new ladder for their own comfort and there it was. It looked out of place against the battered hull and Dani knew she'd have to climb quickly. Her dark skin and black dress would stand out clearly.

The aluminum ladder felt warm to the touch and heat pounded off the side of the boat. She really hoped that whatever the heat would do to the contents of the boat, it wouldn't do it while she was onboard. Even with the wind off the water, it felt ten degrees hotter on the sticky deck. Dani ducked down, water slicking her way as she crab-walked to the front of the boat where the wheelhouse jutted up under a tattered canopy.

She found the trap door to the hold between a cooler and a pile of ropes. The sight of a padlock made her swear until she saw the lock wasn't fastened. It was just looped through the hasp to keep the hold door shut. It seemed like a pointless thing to do. The explosives weren't likely to walk themselves out, were they?

Dani didn't care why the Wheelers did what they did. This close, all she could think of was how satisfying it would be to see the boat sinking into the channel waters, maybe get a glimpse of the anger and panic on Bermingham's face as he watched his big deal go down to the deep. Maybe she'd get to flip them all off as she and Choo-Choo drove over the bridge.

The thought made her smile.

Until she opened the hold.

Then all she could do was gag.

The smell was staggering. Ammonia and mildew and some kind of cheesy smell and rust all rising up in an eye-watering funk that made Dani fall back against the deck. She coughed, turning her head for the breeze that did little to dissipate the stench. Good lord, she thought, were these fertilizer bombs?

The heat only intensified the smell but Dani was determined to scuttle this boat. She wished she'd worn a bandanna or something to cover her nose. She held her breath as she climbed down the steps into the hold, feeling around in front of her for a string Choo-Choo had told her would probably be the light switch. Her fingers found the string and she pulled, reminding herself to breathe through her mouth before she fainted.

When the light came on, she forgot the smell.

She forgot to breathe.

Packed into the hold of the *Pied Piper*, covering every square inch of the filthy wet hold, were children. A dozen? More?

Twenty-five prime units.

CHAPTER NINETEEN

Dani saw nothing but eyes and hands and scabby knees where the boys and girls crouched and lay against each other. None of them could be older than ten. Some of them were naked; all of them were filthy. Not one of them made a sound.

Children. Bermingham was buying children. From the Wheelers.

Her butt hit the stairs as her mind tried to take in what she saw. What could she do? She had no boat, no way to get these kids off the *Pied Piper*.

The Pied Fucking Piper.

It wasn't the smell that made it hard to breathe now. It was rage. She didn't care about getting away. She didn't care about Tom Booker or Mr. Randolph or Bermingham. All that mattered now was finding a way to get these kids off this boat.

And making everybody pay for it.

"I'm going to get you out of here."

Her voice was loud in the echoing hold but only a few of the children seemed to hear her. Water sloshed against the outside of the boat, doing nothing to cool the space. They had to move. There was nothing to be done down here. They had to move.

She hurried back up to the wheelhouse. She knew less than nothing about boats, but how much different from cars could they be, right? Steering wheel, motor.

Ignition.

Shit. She had no keys. A quick search over the panels and broken radio and around the sticky floor produced nothing but a splinter in her thumb and something nasty stuck to her arm she wouldn't investigate. There was no way Dani was stealing this boat.

She pounded her fists against the panel of dials, wanting to scream. What could she do? Nothing from here. She had to get back to shore. And do what?

How about calling the FBI? The Feds were so interested in her, maybe they could actually do some good.

But first she had to tell those kids she was leaving them. She had to tell them she was leaving them in the hands of Juan and Joaquin Wheeler, who had taken them from God knows where to trap them in that filthy stinking hole to face a future in the hands of Bermingham.

Dani steadied herself against the railing of the boat. Her head spun from the heat and the anger and the helplessness of it all. Her thoughts struggled to line up, to make some sense of what came next. She had to get past the Wheelers and Bermingham.

She wanted to kill them. She hated them.

Want and hate. That was all she had.

She didn't hear the motor of the dinghy until it nearly reached the trawler. Ducking down below the railing, she caught a glimpse of Juan's greasy head as he steered the little boat toward the ladder. She had to get out unseen. Dani had one foot over the back railing before she realized she'd left the hold open.

He'd know someone had been there. Who knew what he'd do then. She had to lock the children back in that darkness.

XXX

3:30pm, 106° F

"Mr. Vincente wants his money in cash."

"That's bullshit." Bermingham slouched back in his chair. "We had a deal."

"Mr. Vincente is changing the deal."

Oren watched Juan and Bermingham pretending to be cool around the low bar table. Peg and Rolly sat sullenly at the service end of the bar where they'd been ordered to sit. From where he and Caldwell sat at the middle of the bar, in clear sight of Joaquin and his gun, he could just make out the lengthening shadows on the deck. Bermingham's thug Ned stood at the doorway to the deck, keeping an eye on the boat.

"I want to talk to Vincente. Get him on the phone."

"Mr. Vincente said he wants me to handle the arrangements. Mr. Vincente says he no longer feels comfortable with a wire transfer. Mr. Vincente feels that, that . . ." Oren could see Juan struggling to remember his boss's words, invoking his name like a magical spell, ". . . that wire transfers can be compromised and traced. Mr. Vincente wants the payment in cash."

"That's not going to happen. That's impossible."

Juan smiled. "That's another reason we came a couple hours early. To give you time to make it possible. Mr. Vincente says you're a real capable guy."

"I can't just pull a hundred K out of my ass."

"Yeah about that," Juan let out one of his squeaky giggles. "Mr. Vincente says the price went up. Double. In cash."

Bermingham's fingers ghosted over his gun that sat on the table and Juan leered at him. "Remember, I gotta go back to the boat and call Mr. Vincente to let him know you're playing nice. I don't call, the boat goes boom."

Bermingham leaned over the table, his meaty forearms covering the distance to Juan. "What makes you think I'm going to pay double for merchandise that's been sitting in this heat? In an hour it's going to be worthless to me. I won't be able to sell it to anyone."

"Then maybe you'd better hurry up, huh? It ain't getting any cooler out there."

Bermingham fell back in his seat, shifting his gaze to Ned, who stood silently in the doorway. The two men considered each other for a moment before Ned gave an almost imperceptible nod. Bermingham sighed.

"Okay. Tell him we'll do it. Cash. One-fifty."

"Two hundred."

"One-fifty or I walk and he can try to peddle his shit after you sail it back to whatever hellhole you got it from. Another couple hours in this heat he won't be able to trade it for a hand job from a dock whore." The Canadian rose from his chair, pulling out his phone. "I've got to call my people. It's going to take a little time to get that cash."

"I'll go give Mr. Vincente the good news." Juan stood too. "I'll leave you in the care of my brother. There's just one more little matter than needs to be taken care of."

Bermingham scowled. "What now? Gas money?"

"Insurance." Juan pulled his piece and pointed it toward the bar where Oren sat. "There's a Fed here. I know it. You know it. Mr. Vincente knows it. That's got to be taken care of before any of this goes down."

"I'll take care of it."

"Take care of it now. No deal otherwise."

Bermingham looked up from his phone, seeing the way Juan and Joaquin held their weapons, itching to start shooting. "I said I'll take care of it. I'm taking him with me when I go. We're going to have a nice long chat on the water on the way to my ship. If he's very, very cooperative, he may live long enough to see international water."

Oren felt Caldwell stiffen beside him.

"Now or no deal."

"I have questions for him."

Juan didn't move. Bermingham swore, shaking his head in disbelief, and walked over to where Caldwell and Oren sat.

Jesus, this was really happening.

Oren felt the wind as the Canadian swung a backhand that knocked Caldwell to the floor onto his face. Caldwell scrambled to get beneath the nearby table but Bermingham's enormous foot on the back of his leg pinned him to the floor.

"We're gonna have us a nice chat about how you happened to be here today, Agent . . ." he looked over his shoulder at Juan, "what's his name?"

"Caldwell." Juan grinned.

"Agent Caldwell."

Caldwell raised his hands over his head, lying very still on the floor. Oren was thankful his friend couldn't see the weapon Bermingham pointed at his back.

"Now this is going to hurt, Agent Caldwell. It's going to hurt a lot. It's going to register on the Richter scale of hurt, but you be still, okay? You stay nice and still and I'll make sure it doesn't hurt long once you answer my questions. First, though, I've got to make this deal. I have people to answer to, just like you."

The shot deafened Oren for a second. He wished it had deafened him longer. Caldwell screamed, curling up on himself as blood flooded the floor of Jinky's.

"I'll go call Mr. Vincente." Juan headed down the steps to the dock.

Bermingham didn't look at Ned as he went back to the table. Joaquin grinned. Oren could only sit there, watching his friend bleed.

XXX

She couldn't hold her breath. She'd jumped from the railing of the trawler, not even a quarter of the height she jumped from every day after her run, but she couldn't hold her breath. She'd hit the water hard, her body reacting to memories of much, much colder water. Fear, anger, and helplessness choked her. They made her arms clumsy and her legs weak. The tide drew her toward the inlet but every wave seemed to break in her face, every ripple pulled her under until she gasped and choked.

Children. Kids. Little kids in a dark hole to be sold.

She kicked and paddled, spitting salty water and trying to breathe.

Mr. Randolph made a deal with people who sold children.

The water warmed toward the inlet. She was on the wrong side. She was on Jinky's side.

Bermingham had kissed her. She'd kissed *him*. Bermingham bought children.

Seaweed wrapped itself around her fingers, making her want to scream, and she heard the chug-chug of the water at the mouth of the inlet. Broken boards and jagged pieces of fencing hung over the ratty dock hidden behind the clump of bushes. Cracked buoys and rusted cleats rattled against the old boards as the water rose and fell. The screwdriver around her neck caught on the edge of the outer plank as she pulled herself up onto the dock, spitting out mouthfuls of hot sea water.

XXX

Oren heard coughing. After decades on the quiet island, Oren could pick out sounds others never heard. It was easier to hear now that Caldwell had grown quiet. Oren didn't want to think about that. He listened to the new sound. He knew that cough. Dani used to cough like that when she'd started swimming the channel. He hadn't heard it in months, not since she'd gotten so much stronger.

Dani was way too tough to cough like that now.

Ned must have heard it too because he came to attention, moving to the edge of the deck to look toward the water. Joaquin moved to the doorway to look.

"It's nothing," Ned said.

"I'll go check it out." Joaquin waved his gun around at each of them. Nobody seemed to care. Oren sure didn't. "You all stay here. If I see any sign of anyone fucking around, you all die. You understand?"

X X X

4:11pm, 107° F

The wood scraped her knees as she crawled across the old planks, her hands fumbling over the debris gathered there. When Joaquin Wheeler pushed aside the waxy shrub, she sat back on her heels and looked up.

His upper lip drew back in what passed for a smile; his good eye fixed on her. She flipped her wet hair back from her face and smiled at him.

"Hi Joaquin."

"You're not supposed to be here."

"Yeah, I get that. I was just curious, you know?" She held eye contact with him but made note of the gun hanging from his right hand. She got to her feet slowly, keeping her own right hand behind her back. "I was wondering what the big deal was. Kids, huh? I wouldn't have taken you for a pedo. You always seemed too"—her gaze roamed over his lumpy form—"big a man. Guess you never know, huh?"

He wheezed out a protest. "That ain't for me. It's just business. Big business. Juan maybe likes a little of that, but I like my ass a little older, you know what I mean?"

192

She bit her lip, inching closer to him. The wet dress clung to her and she saw Joaquin's good eye follow tracks of water across her skin. She cocked her hip, keeping her right arm behind her so her body eclipsed the rusted boat cleat she gripped.

A loud whine sounded that she knew was just in her head. It was blood rushing through her veins, pounding at her to move, to strike. But she didn't. Mental boxes opened; mental boxes closed as she remembered what her father had taught her.

Offer what they want in one hand; take what you want with the other.

She licked her lips slowly and inched closer.

You do what you have to do until you don't have to do it anymore.

"I saw Juan head back to the boat. I guess that means you're the man in charge." His lip curled more and Dani could see something yellow and dried stuck in the corner of his mouth. "I like to know who's in charge, Joaquin. I like to be good to people who can be good to me." She stood close enough to smell his breath that sped up the closer she came. "Will you be good to me, Joaquin?"

Saliva bubbled on his lips when he spoke. "You gonna be good to me?"

Dani dropped her gaze in a show of girlish modesty. The gun hung forgotten from his hand. Looking up from under her lashes, she pulled down the neckline of the dress, exposing her left breast. Joaquin's breath caught as she slid her hand over her skin, her fingers playing over her nipple.

Offer what they want with one hand.

"Touch me, Joaquin. Show me who I belong to."

She saw his right hand start and saw him realize he still held a gun. He did what she knew he would do, what she counted on. He raised his left hand to her breast, bending his head forward and opening up the side of his neck.

Take what you want with the other.

She swung the boat cleat hard. Bits of rotten deck wood still clung to the bottom, attached by a long, exposed screw that buried itself in the flesh of Joaquin's cheek. He staggered at the blow and she had to yank the cleat free. As he fell, she kneed his groin and brought the cleat down hard again on the back of his neck. He tried to yell but she backhanded him with the edge of the metal, sending him sprawling. Not giving him a chance to get his bearings, she dropped heavily on both knees onto his stomach, forcing the air from his mouth in a bloody burst.

He jerked beneath her and she swung the dripping cleat back over her head for another blow and felt a tight hand on her wrist, stopping her. A white canvas sneaker pressed the bloody man's face against the dock.

Tom.

"What's this, Dani?"

"You." She let him pull her to her feet and she did nothing to hide her disgust. "This is who you are? This is who you work with now? You sell kids? You sell babies?"

He held her arm, his eyes wide. When Joaquin groaned, he moved his foot down and pressed it against the man's bloody throat, cutting off the sound. "What are you talking about?"

"That's why you're here, right? To protect this deal?" She could see the words hitting home and she desperately wanted to bury the cleat in his skull. "Is that what kind of man you are? Selling little kids to pervs to play with? You're nothing like I thought you were. You're not a man at all."

Something shifted in his face, something that turned his beautiful eyes hard and alien. If it hadn't been for the adrenaline, Dani might have been afraid, but she was past fear now.

"What children?"

She looked over her shoulder at the *Pied Piper*. "On that boat. Twenty-five of them. Alone with Juan Wheeler to be sold to Tucker

Bermingham. So which one of them hired you? Huh? Which pedophile signs your paycheck?"

His grip on her wrist tightened to the point of pain, but Dani refused to flinch. He bared his teeth, staring past her toward the boat. She could feel her fingers tingling before he came back to himself, dropping her wrist as if just noticing he held it. Dani didn't know which was more terrifying—the look of unfiltered rage that had glowed on his face or the ease with which he put it away.

He slid his fingertips over the red marks on her wrist, following her fingers down to the bloody cleat. "Don't hit him in the forehead. It's too hard to break. Bring it down on his nose; let the screw go into his brain."

Dani nodded.

He dropped his gaze from hers. His hands moved slowly. With care, he lifted the neckline of her dress to cover her breast. Then he slipped into the water.

CHAPTER TWENTY

Bermingham surprised Oren by throwing him a bar towel when Joaquin left the room. "Put pressure on the wound. He'll live."

He dropped to his friend's side quickly, relieved to see Caldwell conscious and calm. The blood had slowed.

"No talking."

Oren nodded reassurance to Caldwell while Bermingham paced the floor. Ned stayed in the doorway, scanning the grounds.

"What the hell is taking so long? Where's Joaquin?"

Ned nodded toward the water. "He went that way to check out the noise."

"And?"

"And nothing yet. He went behind those shrubs. There's been no noise, no shots. No boats on the water. Nobody walking around. Maybe he's taking a leak."

"This is wrong." Bermingham shook his head and Oren could hear the anxiety in his voice. "Something's up. We've got to call this. They're going to blow that boat. Vincente is going to fuck us."

"Give it another fifteen minutes," Ned said. "Give Juan a chance to tell Vincente we're going with cash."

Bermingham stared down into the inlet, frowning. "Where's Dani? Where's that blond kid? Have you seen him?"

"I left him at that shed where she sleeps. He's sitting right there. Hasn't moved."

Bermingham stomped over to Oren and pressed his gun to the side of his face. "Tell me where Dani is."

"How should I know?" Oren looked up as much as possible past the muzzle.

"Tell me where she is!"

"How?" Oren asked. "I didn't put a fucking bell on her. She comes and goes as she pleases. You're the one who's so tight with her. Aren't you the one pulling her strings?"

Bermingham stared at him for several beats before lowering his gun.

"This is bullshit. Ned, keep an eye on these two. If either of them moves, shoot them. If anything moves, shoot it. If this deal turns to shit . . ."

X X X

4:22pm, 107° F

Dani stood over Joaquin's bloody body. He labored to breathe, red bubbles popping on his nose and mouth. The cleat weighed a thousand pounds in her hand. She didn't need to kill him. She needed to get out of there, to find a phone, to get someone who could get those kids off that boat. But Joaquin Wheeler still breathed and that meant he could still be a danger.

And she wanted to kill him.

She had to get to Choo-Choo, find some way to get him out of there too. If Bermingham realized the law was on its way, he'd kill everyone. He'd kill Mr. Randolph. She didn't want to care about that but she did. The people she needed to worry about were herself, those kids, and Choo-Choo. Everyone else would have to take care of themselves.

But the cleat felt so heavy in her hands.

It felt so good smashing into Joaquin's skin.

"Put it down."

Bermingham stepped through the gap in the shrubbery, his gun trained on her. Dani knew the Canadian was far too savvy to fall for any adolescent seduction scene, especially now, standing over a bloody Wheeler. He kept the gun on her as he crouched, feeling for Joaquin's pulse. "Shit," he muttered, moving his fingers through the mess. "Shit."

"Dani, I swear to God . . ." He straightened and grabbed her by the arm, squeezing it until she had to drop the cleat. "If you have fucked this deal, I swear to God, Dani, I will blow a hole in you big enough to drive through."

"Fuck you."

"You have no idea what you're screwing with, what you're risking."

"Fuck you." She let him jerk her forward. "You fucking pedophile. You filthy panty raider. Get your rocks off on little boys' tighty-whities. Is that it?"

"Shut your mouth," he hissed in her ear, but Dani wouldn't keep it down.

"You like 'em small, Bermie? Huh? Can't push 'em around when they're grown up, right?"

She didn't know what she said, she just knew it felt right to scream. It felt righteous. She barked at him, laughed at him. When he slapped her face, she spit blood on his shirt. When he jerked her forward she tilted her head back and screamed.

"Tucker Bermingham buys little boys to fuck!"

When he put his hand over her mouth, dragging her, she bit his fingers hard enough to break the skin until finally, when he slammed her head against the deck post of Jinky's, she slid into blackness, crumpling onto the gravel.

XXX

4:36pm, 107° F

Oren heard footsteps coming up the stairs to the deck. The blond came through first, propelled by a kick from Bermingham. Oren couldn't tell who looked angrier, the kid or the Canadian, and he didn't care. All he could focus on was the limp body of Dani draped over Bermingham's shoulder, blood dripping from her forehead. Ned hopped to attention, grabbing the blond and holding him at gunpoint. Bermingham lowered Dani to the floor. Oren didn't miss the way he cradled her head.

"Get Juan on the phone." Bermingham yanked the screwdriver from around Dani's neck, tossing it several feet away. "I don't know who she's working for. I don't know what's going on, but Joaquin is dead. If she's fucked us, if Vincente sent her to fuck us, she's going to regret drawing her next breath. Get him on the phone."

"I've been trying," Ned said. "While you were gone. No answer."

"Shit!" Bermingham grabbed the blond. Although tall, the kid had none of the Canadian's bulk. He also didn't have a gun and so didn't resist when Bermingham pressed the weapon underneath his jaw. "Who do you work for?"

"Casper van Dosen."

"Who?"

Oren shook his head. Did this kid have a death wish?

"Casper van Dosen. I was supposed to start tonight on the sunset cruise." He rolled his eyes toward the deck. "I suspect I've missed my launch. No chance you're hiring, eh?"

"Shit!" Bermingham threw the kid toward the bar where Oren sat willing himself into invisibility. The kid stumbled, falling to one knee before straightening up and settling onto a barstool. It was an odd thing to see. The kid was graceful, the stumble out of place. It was then Oren saw what Bermingham didn't.

He'd kicked the screwdriver closer to Dani.

Dani's hand slid over the handle as Bermingham stood with his back to them all, scowling at Ned. The kid sat half-perched on the edge of the stool, his long fingers wrapped around the stool's leg on his right side. Oren knew all the signs of a bar fight when he saw them.

Oh shit.

Caldwell huffed out a soft breath, a quiet protest, trying to get Oren's attention. The agent obviously saw it too and thought it a bad idea. Oren tried to elbow the kid but he brushed off the gesture, adjusting his grip on the stool.

Oren steadied his breathing. They were all going to get shot.

X X X

4:27pm, 107° F

Booker hated the water. He always had. He could swim; it wasn't that. He hated the bottomlessness of it, the sensation of drifting with no solidity. He hated the sound of his pulse in his ears and the loud rush of breath when he broke the surface. Plus he hated getting his knives wet. Still, his dislike of the water paled in comparison to the eruption of loathing within him when Dani had told him what was on the boat.

He saw her in his mind, wet and covered in another man's blood. Her breast.

The shiver that ran through him almost made him gulp water and Booker shut the thought down. There would be plenty of time to fully explore the memory later.

He had a job to do.

For obvious reasons Booker wasn't a religious man or even a spiritual one, but he did have an animal's faith in the rightness of life. He believed he was lucky, that more often than not he was in the right place at the right time for the right reasons. Take Florida, for example. He hated it. He hated wearing shorts; he hated seeing Dani being touched by another man; he hated swimming. A less optimistic man might feel that life conspired against him, throwing all those loathsome things at him at once, but not Booker. He understood the purpose of hate.

When acknowledged and understood, there was no deadlier weapon.

And of all the things he'd hated so far on this trip, nothing came close to how much he hated what was happening on that boat.

X X X

Juan didn't see him when he climbed off the ladder. Not at first. As Booker stepped around the clutter on deck to reach the wheelhouse, he saw why. Juan sat perched on the edge of the captain's seat, his pants around his knees, talking on his phone to someone named Vincente, while his eyes roamed over a small girl standing in front of him. Booker assumed it was a girl. The dirty little shorts didn't give much of a clue but one side of her black hair hung in a tattered pigtail.

Juan smiled as he ended the call. He must have caught movement from the corner of his eye because he jumped to his feet, knocking the little girl down as he struggled to get his pants up. Booker held up his hands and smiled.

"It's okay! It's okay! Don't shoot." He stepped closer and leaned against a deck chest, his arm draped over a thick coil of rope. "Dani sent me. About the kids."

He watched Juan scowl, thinking, and then relax. "What did she want?"

"To give you this."

Juan never saw the metal hook that Booker pulled from the coil of rope.

XXX

It didn't take long to get him in place. Booker had been careful not to hit him in the temple. He just wanted to stun the little man, not kill him. Not yet. With both hands tied over his head on the canopy of the wheelhouse, his clothes stripped off and his filthy underwear shoved into his mouth to silence his cries, Juan looked just about ready to be woken up.

But first things first.

Booker crouched down to be face-to-face with the dark-eyed girl. She didn't look afraid. He wasn't entirely sure she knew he was there.

"Do you speak English?"

She stared into his eyes and he saw her focus. She nodded.

"Where are the others?"

She turned to look at the trap door fastened with the open padlock. Booker nodded, removed the lock, and opened the hatch.

He knew that smell. If it smelled less of salt water and more of dogs, it would have smelled exactly as he remembered it.

"Come on out. Come on."

He helped one tiny person after another out of the hold. Some could barely walk. None spoke. Booker saw the way they clung to each other, holding each other up as they breathed in the hot, fresh air, squinting against the lowering sun. When the hold was empty, he shut the hatch. Twenty-five pairs of eyes stared at him.

"I'm not sure how I'm going to get you off this boat. I don't see any reason to lie to you. We'll look for life rafts in a minute. Maybe life preservers. We'll figure that out, okay? But first there's this." He looked from face to face. "When you get to shore, when the police find you and send you home, you're going to talk to counselors and doctors and people who will tell you how to feel about this. No matter what they say though, you're going to wake up in the middle of the night frightened, remembering what's happened to you up to now."

He stood and drew the serrated blade from his waistband. "I want you to watch this. All of it. Afterwards you can tell the police or not, whatever you feel comfortable with, but watch all of this. And months from now, when you wake up frightened, reliving all they've done to you, you tell yourself the rest of the story. You tell it all the way to the end, okay?"

He turned to Juan, tapping him on the cheek to wake him. Juan blinked, shaking his head, trying to focus. When he saw Booker, saw that he was naked and tied, he panicked, twisting and screaming out from behind his filthy gag. When he saw the knife, his bladder gave way.

Booker looked over his shoulder. Twenty-five sets of eyes saw everything.

He smiled. "Let's get started."

CHAPTER TWENTY-ONE

4:40pm, 107° F

Oren couldn't believe they were going to try something. He had to be misunderstanding what he saw. Bermingham and Ned were armed and nervous. Dani had a screwdriver, the kid a chair. Oren knew the shotgun sat loaded and ready on the other side of the bar but from where he sat, it might as well be across the inlet. He glanced down at Caldwell, who gave him a worried look.

The two Canadians stood at the doorway to the deck, squinting into the setting sun. Oren had stared at that scene for twenty years. At this time of day, all they were going to get was retina burn.

Ned shook his head. "You're right. We've got to call it. It's got to be over a hundred and ten on that boat. We've got to get them off."

Choo-Choo made a cluck of disapproval. "Don't like your boy-ass baked?"

"Shut up," Bermingham snapped, but the blond ignored him.

"I'd think the heat would keep them tender, make them more malleable. Let's not pretend you like to diddle children because you like their feisty spirits."

Bermingham pointed his weapon at Choo-Choo. "Shut your fucking mouth."

Ned pushed his arm down. "Ignore him. We don't have time for this. They've got no phones. If Vincente's waiting for a signal from them, we're running out of time. Let's call it."

Bermingham swore again and pulled out his phone with his free hand. He walked while he dialed. "Yeah, Taxi Eight-Fourteen. Abort the minnow. Repeat, abort the minnow. We have word the target is hot, twenty-five souls still aboard. Go now. Use extreme caution. The target may be hot." He banged the phone against his forehead. "And for fuck's sake, hurry up."

He shoved his phone back into his pocket. Oren heard the kid suck in a breath and saw the instant Bermingham made his mistake. Without looking he stepped just inches away from Dani's arm, his toe brushing the edge of the screwdriver. Oren didn't think she even opened her eyes; she moved too quickly for him to tell. All he saw was the screwdriver disappearing into the top of the Canadian's foot hard and fast, more of the long metal vanishing from sight than should have been possible. Oren knew what that meant.

She had nailed his foot to the barroom floor.

He screamed and jerked but she leveraged herself on the spike to snap her legs up and out, nailing Bermingham in the crotch. Dani was nothing but legs, kicking and swinging, hitting any inch of flesh she could reach as the blond kid swung the barstool hard and heavy, knocking the bigger man off his free foot, his trapped foot causing his knee to twist at an unnatural angle. Bermingham's gun flew, Ned shouted, and Oren surprised himself with the revival of his old "leaping behind the bar" skills. He had the shotgun up and out and aimed at Ned. The kid had Bermingham's gun pointed the same direction.

The whole scene had taken only seconds.

Bermingham clutched his leg, trying to right himself. Dani grabbed the barstool from the kid, swinging the heavy oak seat like it weighed nothing. Funny, Oren thought, adrenaline making his ears ring, he'd never noticed just how toned Dani's arms were.

"Put down your weapons." Ned sounded calm, looking from Oren to the kid, keeping his gun trained on the old man with the shotgun. "Neither one of you is good enough to beat me. I can take you both out with a headshot before either of you gets me in your sights. Don't test me."

Oren thought he probably spoke the truth. Oh well.

Dani hefted the stool over Bermingham's head. "Did you know?" The Canadian fell back on the ground. "Did I know what?"

"Not you. Mr. Randolph. Did you know what was on that boat?"

It took a second for Oren to realize she was speaking to him, another second to be able to take his eyes off of Ned's gun. "No. I still don't know."

"It's little kids. They're selling little kids."

"He knew," Bermingham said. "He's done business with the Wheelers for years."

"What?! I didn't know, Dani." Oren could see in her eyes that she needed to decide if he was telling the truth. The idea that she could doubt him about something like that made him forget about the gun, forget about the bleeding men in front of him. "Jesus, Dani, you think I knew? You think I'd allow that? What kind of man do you think—"

He knew the instant he made his own mistake, letting the gun drop down toward the bar.

Ned's bullet threw him back against the mirror, glass and liquor exploding out behind him as his head smashed against the shelves. He couldn't understand why he could see his feet until he realized the shot had blown him back onto the cooler, seating him in a puddle of blood and rum. Then he felt the pain.

He couldn't hear the screaming for a while. Time got funny, everyone moving but nobody leaving their spot.

Holy shit, it hurt.

XXX

Dani almost dropped the stool when Ned shot Mr. Randolph. Choo-Choo flinched and as he'd promised, Ned had his weapon trained on him in no time. She heard Caldwell shouting to his friend but Mr. Randolph didn't say anything. He just panted, clutching his bloody shoulder, staring wide-eyed at nothing.

"Stop! Stop!" Bermingham held up his hands, screaming at Ned. He pointed to Choo-Choo. "Put your weapon down."

Dani saw that high color on Choo-Choo's face. He'd told her the next time he got shot would be the last time. He obviously meant it because he didn't turn away from Ned.

Bermingham sat back on his elbows, his face sweaty with pain and effort. She knew that leg had to be alive with agony, the twist of his knee getting no relief with his foot nailed to the floor. But he looked at her like he controlled the room, like she was the one trapped. She wanted to kick him.

"Don't do this, Dani. Put the chair down. Tell your buddy to put down the gun."

"Fuck you, Bermingham. You have no idea what I can do."

"Is that right?" He smiled at her. "You think you're protected? Huh? Let me tell you something. Whoever is pulling your strings, whoever's keeping your secret, they won't be able to help you here. If you're the reason twenty-five stolen kids die on that boat, nobody will be able to protect you."

"Protect me?" She laughed. "You think someone's protecting me?"

"I do. I don't know who they are but they don't have enough juice for this. Not this."

Choo-Choo spit on the floor. "Oh look, Dani," he said with a sneer. "Another big shot on the field. Another all-powerful force. Gee, I hope we don't get in trouble for this."

She held her friend's stare long enough to see he shared her rage. He was willing to go all the way with this. Ned could shoot her or he could shoot Choo-Choo but he couldn't get them both at once. She reared back with the stool. "You're nothing but a two-bit child-molesting thug."

"No, Dani, no!" Bermingham held his hands out to block the blow. "I'm with the FBI. I'm with the FBI!"

"Bullshit!" Mr. Randolph sputtered, making Dani jump. His voice was reedy with pain. "He shot Caldwell. I saw him. He shot him."

"If I hadn't, Juan would have done it for me. I grazed him, a flesh wound." Bermingham looked from Dani to Caldwell. "You think I couldn't have killed him? I was a foot away. It was the only way to keep him alive."

Caldwell pounded on the floor with his fist. "It's true, Dani. It's true. Bermingham . . . he told me." He tried to sit up but failed. "He said I'd feel it on the Richter scale. My boss, my SAC, is Tomblin Richter. That's when I knew. Dani," his voice trembled. "Don't."

Bermingham looked up at her. "I swear to you, Dani. I'm here with the FBI. Joint task force. We've been trying to get Vincente on human trafficking and this was it. We need the Wheelers alive to turn state's evidence against Vincente. Without them, the case falls apart. We need the Wheelers alive. You already killed Joaquin. Don't make this any worse."

X X X

Oren blinked sweat out of his eyes, watching Dani holding that heavy stool. Damn, she was strong. Through the pain and shock, he tried to make sense of what was happening. Caldwell said Bermingham and Ned were FBI; Caldwell believed them. That made it true, right?

He could see the doubt all over Dani's face. He wanted to keep watching, to help somehow, but Oren could feel darkness washing up around the edges of his mind.

Dani should believe Bermingham. Put the chair down. The Canadian seemed to be saying something along those lines. Oren struggled to focus.

"Listen to me, Dani. I'm with the FBI. You know, the good guys."

Funny, Oren thought before he drifted off, Dani sure looked like she wanted to smash him with that chair.

X X X

"You know, the good guys."

That was the last thing she heard. The adrenaline-and-rage whine in her ears grew deafening and in her mind's eye she could see how beautiful the heavy wooden chair would look smashing through Bermingham's pretty, pretty face.

The good guys.

Her muscles sang as she swung the stool back, the air alive with noise and light. Then the chair was gone, her hands were empty. Choo-Choo had yanked the stool out of her hands, grabbing her wrists. Was he speaking? No. He just shook his head.

The men with the guns and body armor were speaking. Flooding the deck. Aiming their guns at her.

Shit.

CHAPTER TWENTY-TWO

Dade County Jail, Miami, Florida
Friday, August 23
2:18am, 79° F

"Take the cuffs off of her. She's not under arrest."

Dani didn't bother to thank the officer who uncuffed her. Nobody had spoken a word to her since they'd put her in the holding cell. Bermingham swung on crutches, lowering himself into the chair opposite her at the scarred metal table. He waited until the door closed to speak.

"Talk to me. It's just us now."

Dani nodded at the mirrored glass behind him. "Just you and me and the entire police force of the state of Florida."

"No," he said. "It's just us. Cameras are off; the room is empty. I made sure of it."

"Well aren't you a big shot? Whoever you are."

He folded his hands in front of him, looking her straight in the eye. "My name is James Tucker. I'm a senior agent in the Royal Canadian Mounted Police."

"You're a Mountie?"

He grinned, those dimples popping out just as deep as she remembered them. "Want me to put on the hat?" She couldn't help but laugh. It was just too absurd.

"I've been undercover as Tucker Bermingham for two years, targeting human trafficking coming up from the Caribbean. We've had our eye on Vincente for a long time and finally got him to bite. It wasn't easy putting this operation together, teaming up with the FBI. It took special permission from the Attorney General. I'm here operating under an MLAT, Mutual Legal Assistance Treaty."

She sighed. "Should I be taking notes?"

"Maybe I should be." He tapped his fingers on the manila file folder in front of him. "We went through a lot of trouble to set this up. We didn't know how wide Vincente's team was on this job. We knew the Wheelers—they were a no-brainer—but we had to be sure how involved your boss was, and his friend, Caldwell. We had to be sure the local office kept him out of the loop. We didn't want him getting wind of the operation in case he was dirty."

"Was he?"

"No. We've come to believe your boss wasn't either."

She smirked. "Shame about having to shoot them."

"The only thing we couldn't figure out was you. We had background checks on everyone within twenty miles of Jinky's. I knew what Oren Randolph's piss smelled like."

"Vodka, I'd wager."

He ignored her. "When I heard Juan Wheeler say your name over the phone, we searched for you too. Danielle Kathleen Britton of Flat Road, Oklahoma. That's all we got."

She smiled, hiding her damp palms underneath the table. "Good, clean living."

"And then the Attorney General of the United States of America called my boss and told us to stop running a background check on you. No reason. No options. We were going into this whole operation with a great big question mark right in the middle of it. Two years of my life, Dani, I've done nothing but eat, sleep, and breathe Simon Vincente. We were this close to getting him. He's never been this hands-on in a deal, and he was ours. We could have turned the Wheelers and he would have been ours."

"And all you had to do was put the lives of twenty-five little kids at risk."

"Don't kid yourself." He leaned across the table into her face. She didn't back off. "Twenty-five kids is an afternoon to Vincente. He's got kiddie porn rings on every continent. He sells kids the way Tim Horton's sells doughnuts. Human life is nothing to him and we could have had him."

"Could have?" Dani asked. "Won't Juan play nice?"

"Juan? Juan Wheeler?" He opened the file. "He wasn't really in any shape to be interrogated when the agents boarded the boat."

Dani felt her mouth go dry. "Why not?"

Bermingham scanned a sheet of paper. "Let's see, forensics was able to piece together a pretty interesting story from what was left of him. Genitals in his mouth, an eyeball was found in his stomach. You don't even want to know where they found one of his hands. And all of it done peri-mortem. Do you know what that means? It means whoever did that to him, did it while he was alive. Oh, and they did it in front of twenty-five traumatized children."

Dani forced her shoulders to relax. Mental box open. Mental box close.

"Are you waiting for me to burst into tears at the loss of Juan Wheeler?"

Bermingham leaned back in his seat, studying her. "Who are you? It's just you and me now, I swear. I know you killed Joaquin; we wrote it off as self-defense. The blond kid didn't kill Juan. We ran every time scenario on it. There were no boats in the water and he was dry. You were wet. We found your fingerprints on the boat."

"You think I took Juan Wheeler apart? In front of those kids?"

He watched her for a long minute. "No. But I think you know who did. I think you know who we're looking for. 'The man with the beautiful eyes.' That's what one of the little girls said; that's how she described him. And then she gave a pretty accurate description of a spleen removal for a seven-year-old." He leaned forward, lowering his voice.

"Give me a name. Just tell me his name. Nobody needs to know it came from you."

He was good at this, Dani thought. He didn't abuse the dimple power. She could tell him. He would believe her. All she had to do was open her mouth and let two words fall out, three syllables. Easy as pie. And then what?

Tom Booker hadn't paid for his crimes in DC. He'd gotten free health care for them. Would they arrest him for this? For killing Juan Wheeler? For going off their carefully scripted plan? For saving those kids? Bermingham hadn't seen that boat. He hadn't smelled it. Neither had Tom. But that didn't keep him from doing what needed to be done.

She rubbed her thumb over her palm, certain she could still see traces of Joaquin's blood there. She remembered the comforting weight of the rusted cleat. She looked up at Bermingham and kept her mouth shut.

"I can't make you tell me," Bermingham said. "It's been made very clear to my supervisors that I can't make you do anything, you or your blond friend. I can't hold you; I can't charge you with impeding the investigation. I wouldn't anyway. It's over. We're going to have to try for Vincente somewhere else."

He closed his eyes, rubbing his hands over his face, exhaustion in every move. "I don't know who you work for. I don't know who has your back." He dropped his hand to the table and stared at her. "But if you're in business with the man who did that to Juan Wheeler, you are in business with a monster. Whatever they've told you, whatever they've promised you, Dani, believe me. You are on the wrong side."

"Ah yes, good guys and bad guys."

Tucker pulled a card from his pocket and began writing. "I don't know what that means. I don't know a lot, apparently, but I know this. I don't answer to your Attorney General or the FBI or the United States of America, and I don't have any doubts about whether or not I'm a good guy." He slid the card in front of her. "That's my private number. I won't ask any questions. But if you want out, if you decide that whatever hold they've got on you is too heavy, you call me. Me. Not the office. Me. I can get you out."

Dani straightened the hem of her dress as she stood. She didn't touch the card.

"Am I free to go?"

Bermingham nodded and sighed. "Who's going to stop you?"

She got as far as the door. She couldn't meet his eye as she turned back, snatched the card off the table, and pressed it tight to her palm. Then she ran.

X X X

Miami Hilton
4:20am, 71° F

Jimmy Tucker poured himself a scotch from the minibar. He wasn't Bermingham anymore. Not for a while at least. His team was looking into how badly his cover had been blown. Part of him hoped it had been blown straight to hell.

The doctors had told him not to mix alcohol with pain pills but nothing seemed to be touching the hot throbbing ache in his foot. Besides, he was so tired, he'd have welcomed an overdose coma. As long as he woke up in time to catch the early flight back to Montreal, Tucker didn't care what happened to him tonight. Everything he'd brought with him was packed and waiting by the door. He'd told Ned to drag him to the plane if necessary.

He'd just fallen back on the empty bed when someone knocked on the door. Of course. He was tempted to ignore it but years in law enforcement made that impossible.

"Who is it?"

A muffled voice answered back. He was going to have to go to the door.

Hauling himself up onto his crutches, he swore a little oath of evil to Dani Britton for the damage she'd done to his foot. Who knew such a little girl could hammer a screwdriver so hard? He didn't bother putting a shirt on. Whoever wanted to talk to him now would have to accept him in his boxers.

He peered through the peephole. He could make out a pale face under dark hair, a rumpled white button-down shirt and a bad-looking tie. Who needed an FBI badge when the uniform was so regimented? The man must have heard him approach the door because he held up a folder to the peep hole.

"Need your signature." The door muffled his voice. "Sorry."

Tucker threw back the deadbolt and opened the door. The guy apologized again, following him into the room. "Sorry about bothering you so late. I know you're flying out soon. We really need to get these statements filed before we put this to bed. It'll be my ass if not."

"Yeah, yeah, don't worry about it." Tucker swung himself toward the desk under the window. "It never ends, does it? You'd think getting stabbed would be enough, but nope, nothing's real until the paperwork's done."

The guy opened the folder on the desk, rifling through pages before stepping back and handing Tucker a pen. "Sign and initial. You know the drill."

"Yeah." Tucker swung forward, bending down over the desk. The pages didn't look familiar. He flipped one over. It was a rental car contract. "I think you brought the wrong—"

His chin cracked on the edge of the desk as his good leg gave way beneath him. Everything felt wet.

X X X

Booker stepped back from the spray of arterial blood. The serrated blade had sliced both femoral arteries before the big man had even felt the metal. From the way he fell, Booker thought he probably also cut a tendon or two. The fact that he just wore boxer shorts made the job that much easier.

Booker was lucky that way.

He didn't have long. The human body would bleed out in minutes with that kind of damage and he wanted the man to know what was happening.

"I killed Juan Wheeler."

His face was so pale, his legs sprawled uselessly in front of him. He blinked at Booker.

"Why? Why are you doing this?"

"Because you put your hands on Dani." Booker pointed his fingers at the man's wide eyes. "You jabbed at her like this. Do you remember? You barked at her, at Dani. You tried to push her around."

The man licked his dry lips, words difficult. "Who are you? Who is she?"

"She's mine. That's all you need to know."

The man fell back against the floor, his eyes widening and losing focus. The carpet was a mess. Booker collected the file folder and bent down to take the pen from the man's fingers. He made a point of wiping his shoes of any traces of blood before leaving the room.

He didn't want to get the rental car dirty.

CHAPTER TWENTY-THREE

Jinky's Fishing Camp
Redemption Key, Florida
Friday, August 30, 8:45pm, 84° F

The sun had been down over an hour. Casper had docked the party boat at the farthest slip, letting Choo-Choo lead the contingent of tourists up onto the deck for a post-cruise celebration. Peg threw drinks up and down the bar, Dani hauled buckets of beer out to the deck. Angel Jackson sat with some buddies at the far end of the bar and Casper held court with a couple of too-tanned forty-somethings in Michigan shirts. Without anyone making a point of it, two stools at the service end of the bar remained empty, as if they had an energy of their own.

Dani had stayed at Jinky's and Choo-Choo had stayed with her. It hadn't taken much discussion. There simply wasn't anyplace better to go. But Dani hadn't told Choo-Choo about the card, or the phone number with the Montreal area code she had memorized before slipping it behind the door panel of her old Honda. She'd closed the information up in one of her mental boxes, leaving it alone until she felt safe enough to consider what to do with it.

Peg bumped her hip as she dug around in the cooler. "What?" Dani said, grabbing two bottles and straightening up. The bar had gotten quiet. Quieter, at least. The crowd around Casper continued to laugh too loudly. The locals had stopped everything to watch two men move toward the bar.

Mr. Randolph looked ten years older. A wide sling held his left arm close to his body. Dani couldn't help but think how inconsiderate it was that Ned had shot him in his drinking arm. Beside him, Caldwell winced as he maneuvered himself onto the barstool. She could see the outline of bandages underneath his loose guayabera shirt.

Without waiting to be asked, Dani poured Mr. Randolph a vodka over ice with a lime wedge squeezed to death in it. Peg abandoned the margarita she was making and poured something into a tall glass for Caldwell.

One of the Michigan women must have noticed the change in the air because she looked down the bar at the two men. She squinted at Mr. Randolph's sling and scowled at Caldwell's careful movement.

"Well," she said in a voice too loud for the quiet bar, "what happened to you two?"

Caldwell scowled. Mr. Randolph took a sip of his drink before speaking.

"We forgot our safe word."

The woman tilted her head like a confused dog. Nobody spoke until Rolly leaned out the kitchen window.

"Twenty-four?"

All eyes turned to Mr. Randolph.

He nodded. "Twenty-four."

He made circles in the air with his good hand and the locals cheered. Dani started pouring the tequila.

ACKNOWLEDGMENTS

Many thanks to my development editor, David Downing. As always, you make me a better writer even while you make me laugh. Terry Goodman, you'll forever be my Dark Overlord, and I'm very psyched to be kicking off a new journey with Alison Dasho. The whole team at Thomas & Mercer deserves heaps of praise.

Thanks to my agent, friend, and rubber-room renter, Christine Witthohn. Love ya, *chica*.

I wore so many people out, badgering them for their expertise: Lara Nance, who is my *de facto* boating expert; Jamie Whitt for his aviation expertise and tireless enthusiasm; Gordon Ramey, who corrects my gun lingo; and Mike Eden at Eden House at Key West, who put such a friendly face on Florida for us. They did the best they could to get through to me. All mistakes are my own.

I freely stole names from some very nice people to create some not-so-nice characters. Thanks to the real Jim Bermingham, Mr. Shawn Randolph, and Mike Caldwell. I hope you all had fun.

Big love to my family near and far; to Gina, Debra, Tenna, Christy, and Angela—the amazing Hitches I get to call friends; to my fellow WV Writers, BC Babes, and Matera Peeps, especially Liz Jennings, who always has time for me.

ABOUT THE AUTHOR

An avid traveler, S.G. Redling lives and writes in West Virginia.